You've Got Fe-Mail!(TM)

By

Kristin Cranford

This book is a work of non-fiction. Names and places have been changed to protect the privacy of all individuals. The events and situations are true.

ISBN: 1-4140-2458-4 (e-book)
ISBN: 1-4140-2459-2 (Paperback)
ISBN: 1-4140-2460-6 (Dust Jacket)

Library of Congress Control Number: 2004090197

This book is printed on acid free paper.

1stBooks - rev. 03/09/04

CHAPTER 1

I love online dating—thought I wouldn't, but I do. The lesbian dating world is so small that if a friend has a dinner party, all she has to do is move the place setting one seat in order for her new girlfriend to sit next to her.

I had ended a yearlong relationship. I mourned for the appropriate length of time and now needed to branch out and meet single, eligible women. I found the perfect tool to find the woman of my dreams: the Internet!

All I can say is I should have tried it earlier. I posted an ad on love at online lesbian dating in the middle of December. My goal was to correspond with women via e-mail, instant messenger, exchanging photos, and online dating. I wanted to receive and respond to ads and go on actual dates, while my exes came in and out of the experience. I needed to experience the highs and lows of online dating in search of finding true love.

Is this possible, and how long will this take? Can one find true love through online dating, corresponding via e-mail and instant messaging? Is the Internet a tool that links cyber love with physical love, creating an everlasting relationship? This is a diary of a lesbian searching for true love, a girl who would not settle for less, documented it, and shared the experience with the world. Does she find her true love or not?

I was visiting my friend in New Orleans several weeks prior to Christmas. I was on her computer while she was at work, killing time, as I had just seen my ex, my first love, the day before. We hadn't seen each other in over three years. We hadn't dated in over five years. The prior day's meeting was the ending of all communication, a closure that we both needed, and it was long overdue. Our relationship never lasted, as she was not strong enough to live a lesbian lifestyle. I beat my head against a wall for seven years, trying to change her mind. The time had come for me to completely release her from my heart; I want to have a partner who lives and believes in the gay lifestyle, a woman who stands up for what she believes in, what we believe in.

It was difficult seeing her. She and my friend picked me up from the airport, and the three of us went to lunch, just like old times. Not so much. My first love cried the entire time about how much she loved me, how difficult it was seeing me, how she wasn't prepared to feel the way she

1

was feeling, how she constantly thinks about our relationship, how she's sad that she isn't strong enough to live a lesbian lifestyle, how it's too painful for her to be around me because I am a constant reminder of something that she wants but can't have. During lunch, she asked us to take her home, meet her new boyfriend, see how her two boys have grown over the years, and say our final good-byes.

I reluctantly agreed, as I didn't want to end things this way. But I had no choice; with her I never had choices. The boyfriend was nice, the boys had grown. After the pleasantries, I gave her a hug good-bye, turned, and left. My friend and I immediately went to the liquor store and spent the afternoon drinking beer in her back yard, reminiscing about the good old times! Thank goodness for friends.

With that chapter of my life finally closed, I started surfing the Internet to find the woman of my dreams. I came across a woman who lived in Malibu, not too far from where I lived. She looked a lot like my first love, and I was drawn to her immediately. I wanted to send Ms. Malibu an e-mail. You can look at the photos, read the ads, get all juiced up, write an e-mail, and click the send button—but then it stops and tells you that you must become a member to send e-mails! "Hmmm," I thought, great marketing tool. I immediately purchased a six-month membership for $30.00 a month, and I immediately sent Ms. Malibu an e-mail.

I received one response by the time I returned to Los Angeles later in the week. I posted my ad without a photo at first, then posted my photo, and now I can't keep up with all of the lesbians. It's actually a bit out of control, to be honest.

Ms. Malibu sent me a response. We e-mailed back and forth over the Christmas holidays. Due to our busy schedules and the holidays, we both lost interest in one another, and our relationship slowly fizzled out. In the meantime, I met an older woman, Ms. Environmental Scientist. We hit it off immediately, and e-mailed back and forth. One day she I.M.'d me and told me to call her. I didn't, as I am not a phone person, and I was walking out the door for work. I called her later in the afternoon. We talked on the phone a few times after that. Finally we agreed to meet in person, as both of us wanted to cut to the chase.

Last night, I went on a date with Ms. Environmental Scientist. I was a little taken aback at first, as she resembled her photo, yet looked a lot older. I wasn't sure what to expect. We agreed to meet at the Normandy Room, a lesbian bar in West Hollywood. I walked in and searched the bar for her. She was sitting at a table. She recognized me immediately, and

2

watched me scan the room for her. I then glanced over, and there she was, smiling at me.

I approached her, said "Hello," and then sat down. We talked for a few minutes. She went to get us a drink. As she walked towards the bar, my second girlfriend, X-#1 brushed past her, gave me a hug, and sat at a nearby table with her friends. Fortunately, X-#1 knew I was on a blind date. Of course she did, because we are friends and talk daily. Ms. Environmental Scientist returned to the table and we conversed for a few hours, enjoying each other's company. X-#1 eventually made her way over, introduced herself, (she couldn't resist) and then left the bar. There's nothing worse than being on a blind date, with your ex sitting two tables over, critiquing the date you are trying to engage in; but then again, that is normal in the lesbian dating world. I enjoyed Ms. Environmental Scientist's company, yet I was a little timid. We left, grabbed a bite to eat at a local eatery, and then said good night. She walked me to my car. Sensing my hesitation, she didn't press me for a kiss. It was a perfect evening.

I went home and slept in. She called me the next morning and asked me to a movie. I agreed. I was lounging around, surfing the Internet, when I started receiving e-mails from this hot little number in Beverly Hills. I was into what was transpiring, when the telephone rang. Mind you, I have a second date in a few hours with Ms. Environmental Scientist. I picked up the telephone, and who should be calling but X-#2, the ex that I had recently ended things with. She was in the area and needed to talk to me. She came over, we talked, and we ended up in bed! I told her before that happened that I had to leave shortly for a date. She didn't care. She had broken me down. It had been almost three months. It was a nice last sex time for us. No aftermath. She had a hiking date in a few hours, so all was good between us. I showered and she left. Soon after, I went to meet my date from the evening before. We had a good time. She cuddled up next to me in the theater, shoulders touching; it was cute. After the movie was over, we stopped in the restroom—another weird moment for lesbians, because normally your date waits outside for you to return. But not with lesbians; they usually go in as well.

I hate public restrooms; who doesn't? I reluctantly went into the stall, noticed that it wasn't flushed, but was clean. I flushed it and was just about to pee when it started backing up down the back of my pant legs. I about died. I scurried into another stall, quickly left the restroom, and waited for her out front.

Somehow, I was able to leave the theater without her noticing that my pants were wet. We arrived at my car and she said, "I was going to try and kiss you good-bye but it's a little busy at the moment." Thankfully, there was a family getting into the car parked next to mine.

I said, "No, that wouldn't be good, but let's go out again later in the week when you return from San Diego." She agreed and left.

"Wheew, that was a close call," I thought to myself as she walked away. I liked her but that was too fast for this kid. The older lesbian could easily take advantage of me, the younger one. I don't want that, but I now know where things stand with her. She wants me. I could sleep with her out of curiosity, but that's not what I am looking for.

I went home. It was Sunday evening and I was exhausted from my weekend activities. I logged onto my computer and noticed an e-mail from Ms. Beverly Hills. She had invited me to her cabin in Big Bear for a weekend of skiing. I didn't accept, but sent a witty e-mail instead. She loved it and sent me an e-mail asking to "converse on the phone." I graciously accepted, but for another evening.

Meanwhile, X-#1 and X-#2 start I.M.'ing me. Then I received an e-mail from Ms. New York. She sent her photo and explained that she traveled to Los Angeles quite a bit. Before I knew it, I had carpal tunnel syndrome from I.M.'ing and e-mailing these women, and it was almost midnight!

I finally ended communication with all of them. I expected an e-mail from Ms. Beverly Hills and Ms. Environmental Scientist in the morning. I love this Internet dating! It's something I would never have thought about myself, but I always knew if I had a good pool to pick from, I would choose wisely.

CHAPTER 2

I had a tough online dating day today. I received the dreaded e-mail from X-#2 professing her love to me, yet understanding where we are at; hence, no guilt here. I didn't respond. Ms. Environmental Scientist left today to go out of town for two days. She e-mailed me that she had a great time, understood my shyness, yet wanted to go out upon her return. Ms. New York I.M.'d me throughout the day. She was freaking out about why I didn't I.M. her back. I ignored her. I am not a big I.M.'er. One can do that when one has options, Sorry, just stating a fact!

Then the Ms. Beverly Hills drama hit. I thought I would be cute and flirty, and started the morning off by inviting her to meet for a drink at Nic's Martini Bar. It seemed like a fun thing to do, since we both lived in Beverly Hills, right? Wrong. Apparently her name has something to do with the bar's address.

The previous evening, I had e-mailed Ms. Beverly Hills' photo to X-#1. X-#1 said that I have poor taste in women and I was seeking her approval for some odd reason. X-#1 looked at the photo, I.M.'d me back, and said "I think I went on a date with her last year." X-#1 said that she remembered that the woman's name started with a C, that she drove a Porsche Boxster, and that I should ask her. I agreed.

Ms. Beverly Hills responded with a witty e-mail. She was being evasive and cute but would not tell me her name. I responded with another e-mail, mentioning that she drove a Porsche Boxster and that her name started with a C. She didn't care that I knew her name; however, she was a bit freaked out that I knew what kind of car she drove. I explained to her what had occurred, but she didn't believe me. She thought I was a stalker!

I was at the end of my rope. I sent her one last e-mail explaining to her my version of what had occurred; the following is the last e-mail that I sent her:

hey,

i am home, so feel free to call me anytime...my home number is —.—.——...this whole mix up thing is weird... i think i see what you thought happened, here it goes...

5

*the email that i sent you this morning when i said we can meet for
1 drink at nic's martini bar in beverly hills tuesday or wednesday... i
have a feeling you may have heard of the place:) ...you thought i
said that because i knew your name was ——?...*

*you must have thought i called your house last night, heard your
name on your answering machine and that i didn't leave a
message... so, it didn't freak you out that i knew your name, but
when i mentioned what kind of car you drove, that scared you...*

*sorry, that was not my intention at all, i had no clue what was going
on, i really just wanted to know your name (i wasn't going to call
you without knowing your name...gheeez)...*

*then i thought it was weird that you would get freaked out about
someone knowing what kind of car you have, but not think it's
weird that they know your name... for the love of trying to meet for
a drink...lol...*

*i only mentioned nic's martini bar because it's in beverly hills, i
mentioned that it was on such and such drive because there is a
bar across the street from the beverly center called nick's and i
wanted you to be clear as to which one i was talking about...am i
close???*

*and then it turns out that you went on a date with my ex-
girlfriend?...*

*i am laughing so hard right now because try telling this story and
people will think you are nuts...*

*we were meant to meet or meant to stop now, you can call me if
you want to?.*

She responded with a few e-mails. Then she called me. We talked
on the phone for several hours. She had a sexy voice. We are meeting for
drinks tomorrow night. I am becoming a phone person, and that is truly
frightening for anybody who knows me!

She did in fact go on a date last year with X-#1. They met online.
Shocking? Not really; this re-emphasizes the smallness of the lesbian
community.

CHAPTER 3

Online dating is not at all what I thought it was! I started my day with X-#2 freaking out, calling, and e-mailing. We regrouped and worked through it all. Ended up with her apparently (not sure I believe this) saying that we are matches on love at online lesbian dating! The ironic part about that is that she and I met through Internet dating several years earlier. We were friends for over one year before meeting in person, as she lived on the East Coast and I lived on the West Coast. This time she freaked when she saw my ad. I tried to prepare her a few days earlier. It ended with me offering to give her a camera for her to post her picture. She apparently is hot for a girl she met at lesbian soccer. I predicted they would be together by March and I'm saying prayers that that is the case! She agreed to not e-mail for quite some time.

I met Ms. Beverly Hills last evening. She was not all that. We had a good date; it lasted only one hour. She was attractive, yet not my type, nor I her type. We were both uncomfortable, but worked through that. I have now learned what the beauty of vodka holds. I was told that I couldn't drink beer on a date because that would look tacky. So now it's vodka and cranberry with a splash of 7Up. Maybe that's why my stomach has been upset this past week.

We met. She thought that I had curly hair from my photo. I don't know why, but she did. We talked. We immediately told each other that there was no love connection going to happen between the two of us. It relieved our uneasiness. She invited me to her upcoming Super Bowl party to meet several of her single friends. She said that I looked like Jewel, the singer. I don't, but she thought so. She spins; she heard that one of my mentors was a terrible spinning instructor. I tried to convince her otherwise, but gave up shortly. We wrapped up our date, walked to the valet, and waited for our cars to be pulled around. Her car pulled up first; we hugged goodbye and went our separate ways.

She is out, but Ms. Environmental Scientist e-mailed me. She wants to get together. Of course she does, but I am not ready for her. We will end up in bed with no future, and I am not looking for more notches on my bedpost at my age.

So it was back to the old drawing board. I went home, logged on, and Ms. New York e-mailed me that she will be in town next month. So *Sex and the City* meets lesbian *Bridget Jones's Diary* ends here for this evening.

Defeated at the moment, but hopeful something will transpire tomorrow. I continue to receive inquires from people that I would never respond to. However, it makes me feel good to be pursued. I think I was meant to be a movie star. Lesbians throwing themselves at me, and I can pick and choose whom I really want to be with!

CHAPTER 4

I last left off with Ms. Beverly Hills at the ending of that relationship, but the beginning of a new friendship. I immediately took up with Ms. New York. It started with a few e-mails back and forth. Then she started I.M.'ing me again. She is a persistent one. She broke me down one evening; after a few drinks, I responded to her I.M.! She is not my type physically. She e-mailed me several photos. She is "New York cute," meaning big curly hair, hoop earrings, aggressive, smart, quick witted, etc. During our I.M., I suggested that we swap apartments for one week, as I have never been to New York and she wants to come to Los Angeles. I am currently reading a book where the lead character does that. So I threw it out there. She liked the idea, but she liked it better if I were in it with her. Before I knew it, we exchanged phone numbers. Suddenly my phone rang, with the caller ID showing "New York Call." We talked for several hours. We had a wonderful conversation. It was all good, but now my phone won't stop ringing!

The well was running dry. No responses interested me. I e-mailed Ms. Environmental Scientist last night, told her that we were just friends and that we had no future. She didn't understand why. She asked me to explain further. I explained that it just wasn't there for me. She e-mailed back that she had gotten back together with her ex and that she was off the dating market. Maybe I sensed it, maybe I did not, and it didn't matter, as I had no interest in her.

I went out last evening and I had a fantastic time! I met the sexiest woman. My friend got her friend's number, as they are supposed to go out sometime next week. Her friends told me to go talk to her, because she was interested in me, but we were in a large group having fun, and to be honest, I was happy observing her; I did not need to engage in conversation. So we shall see what happens. She appeared to be high-maintenance, somebody to sleep with but not to get involved with. She lives in Long Beach, and that is too far for this kid to drive for any woman; that much I do know. But she sure was nice to look at, and it gave me hope that there were cute, single, feminine lesbians out there!

Before I went out last night, X-#2 called me, asking if I was going to the Normandy Room. I said, "Yes, why?" She said that she was going on a date and didn't want any drama. I assured her by repeating what she had told me the other evening when I told her that I was dating: "Los Angeles is such a large city, how in the world would we ever run into one another?" She didn't think that was funny. She said that she would change her plans. I said, "Great, I will be at the Normandy Room and then I will be going to the Abbey. I hope I don't see you. Have a great evening." We hung up, all was good, and I didn't see her the entire evening.

About 9:30 the next morning, I heard a knock at my front door; I answered the door and it was X-#2 wanting to talk some more, or checking to see if I was alone; I'm not sure which one it really was. We talked for about 20 minutes. I finally asked her to leave. She tried to kiss me, hug me, lay in bed, etc. I told her "No," nicely. She was in therapy. She felt guilty about how she treated me and she wanted to get back together. I told her "No"; it doesn't work that way, I would rather be alone. I also know that she has been dating somebody for one month and she is on the edge of either going forward with that relationship or stopping and trying again with me. I told her to go for it. She was not happy. Oh well, her problem, not mine. And then she left.

Lady (the love of my life, my 14-year-old cocker spaniel) and I went in to work on Sunday afternoon. I was working away until X-#1 called me. She told me that she just met a woman who was my type at the Abbey, and to get over there immediately. I left work, dropped Lady off at home and rushed over to meet her. We met the girl, and she was cute. She sat in the back of the bar with her friends while X-#1 and I got our own table out front. We sat in the sun and enjoyed the afternoon. There weren't many cute women. It's mainly a boy bar. Some friends joined us and we had a fun time. I had a blonde willing to dye her hair black for me! Such is the life in the single lesbian dating world sometimes!

CHAPTER 5

This Internet dating stuff is crazy and hard to keep up with, so I must write as it happens and deal later!

I last left off rushing to meet the cute girl at the Abbey Sunday afternoon, and meeting X-#1 for drinks. I walked into the bar and hugged X#1 hello. We went up to the bar and ordered our drinks. As we were waiting, we noticed the cute girl walking out of the bar; of course she was!

X-#1 was correct in that she was cute and definitely my type. The bartender commented that we were acting like men checking her out, and then laughed and walked away. He was correct, we were doing just that. She came back in a few minutes later, walked over and said "X-#1, I'm so glad to see you again. My boyfriend just dropped me off. Why don't you two come join us in the back?"

We said, "Thank you but no, we like it here in the sun." The word "boyfriend" put a damper on things, as I am not into bisexual women, or women with boyfriends, or women with girlfriends for that matter. I am looking for a single lesbian to spend my life with.

We saw her on and off throughout the day. We ended up meeting a slew of people—lesbians from Dallas, Toronto, and Los Angeles. Then I ran into some friends who decided to set me up with their single friend who is a 28-year-old lawyer. Before I knew it, I had a date to meet her Wednesday evening. We all said good-bye and dispersed one by one. I was happy that I was meeting somebody on Wednesday, only three days away!

By the time Wednesday drew near, I was swamped with work, and meeting someone was the last thing I wanted to do. I e-mailed my friend, told her that I was unable to make it, attached a photo of myself, and said that I would love to meet Ms. Lawyer but I didn't know when. She replied saying that was fine; she would forward my photo and e-mail to Ms. Lawyer.

In the meantime Ms. New York has been calling every night. She is a great sport, as I live in Los Angeles and she lives in New York. There is a three-hour time difference and we spend hours talking on the telephone every evening. I conclude that she must have a sleeping disorder or there is a shortage of single lesbians in New York. Either way, we hit it off immediately, but could an East Coast/West Coast thing really work? Friends for sure, lovers I don't know, but we have a great time talking, e-mailing, and I.M.'ing.

We are to meet in person after my work engagement in March. I am staying two extra days in Florida. She is flying down and we are going to Walt Disney World. So who knows? Very brave of shy Kristin, if I do say so myself, but it's something to look forward to!

Ms. Beverly Hills calls and e-mails me that I must come to her Super Bowl party to meet her friend. After hesitation, I finally agree; locked, sealed, no way out. Hate that! Only to find out later that the friend that she wants to set me up with is Ms. Malibu!

I don't like Ms. Malibu. She added several unflattering photos of herself on the Internet, which she must remove soon. It turned me off. I let that go a long time ago. I have something to look forward to tomorrow. Not! Meeting a stranger with whom I have e-mailed back and forth over the previous months; can't recall what we discussed, since I deleted all of the e-mail correspondences. "Eerie" is what I have to say about that. But Ms. Beverly Hills thinks that we should meet, even if just for friendship, and so it is!

Ms. Laguna Beach has taken an interest in me. She e-mailed me her photo. She is very attractive. We e-mail back and forth. I will try to fit her in before I leave for Paris within the next few weeks.

I'm still friendly with Ms. Environmental Scientist. We exchange e-mails weekly. I continue to receive the normal 20 e-mails daily from strangers whom I just don't have the energy, time, or care to e-mail back. Plus, no photos; at this point, no interest! I know that is rude, but I am maxed out. There is only so much time in one day, and to be honest, this online dating is tiresome sometimes.

Love at online lesbian dating has been very interesting, to say the least. I must note that all of these women e-mailed me, except Ms. Malibu, since I e-mailed her and now she is about to enter my life in person. I feel that she has the upper hand. Not sure why, but I will get that back. Ego out of control? Yes, Internet dating can do that to a person.

No love connection at the moment! X#1 I.M.'d me Friday, upset with her current girlfriend. She dragged me to a sex shop to show me what they were arguing about. Only to find out that her girlfriend was on the cover of 80% of the porn movies. Ouch, she wasn't what she appeared to be!

Then X-#2 freaked out last night. I was taking the garbage out back and ran into her. She scared me. I wasn't taking her phone calls, so she came over unannounced. I leaned against my car and listened to what she had to say. She hugged me and tried to kiss me and I said "No." I finally said good night and left. Two minutes later, she called, needing to vent. I listened patiently, but was fed up. I said that I was tired of her calling me, e-mailing me, stopping by when she wanted to—not taking into consideration that it might not be convenient for me! She didn't hear a word I said. I finally said good-bye and hung up the telephone.

CHAPTER 6

I am into Ms. New York, and she me. We last left off with both of us agreeing to exchange CDs. The other day, I came home to a package of CDs that she made me. I reciprocated and sent her several CDs and a lesbian book called *Choices* that I had just finished reading, one that she had requested I send her. We continue talking on the phone until 3:00 a.m. every night, e-mailing, etc. We are meeting in a few weeks. At first I agreed to share a room, but immediately came to my senses; we will have separate rooms. Worst-case scenario, we are definitely friends, so it will be fun regardless if there is a love connection or not. Her favorite movie is *About Last Night.* Whose favorite movie is that, besides mine? That is creepy, as Sister said, but it says something. Not sure what, but I liked her.

Ms. Environmental Scientist moved to San Diego to be with her ex. After two months, she moved back to Los Angeles, because their relationship didn't last. Of course it didn't last.

I need to tell you about the great lesbian Super Bowl party. I called Ms. Beverly Hills on the way to her house and offered to pick up any last-minute items. She said, "ICE, ICE, and more ICE." I picked up the last two 50-pound bags of ice that existed in the city, drove up the canyon, and found her house. Parking was sparse. I circled back around and unloaded everything onto the curb. Found parking. Walked back to the items I left on the curb, realizing that I was about ten minutes from kickoff. I hate to be late. I was anxious to get there.

I grabbed the bags of ice and the other goodies and walked up 15 steep stairs, only to find a dog barking and an old man yelling at me. I was clearly at the wrong house. I dragged my stuff back down the stairs, walked back to my car that was parked up the hill, reread the directions to find that I was correct, or so I thought. I reached for my cell phone to call her, only to learn that cell phones don't work in the canyon. I realized that I must be off by an Avenue or a Park. I wanted to go home at this point, but felt that would be rude. I drove around for about ten minutes until I finally found her house. I was correct in that she lived on the Avenue, not the Park.

I was frustrated, yet relieved. I re-unloaded my stuff and climbed her stairs. When I finally got inside, we hugged each other hello and I politely said, "I need a minute to regroup. I'll be right back." I sat by myself outside watching her dogs run around, and I noticed several women I did not know milling about. I was thinking, "What have I gotten myself into?"

14

I regrouped, grabbed a beer, and started mingling with the others. I had worn my cargo pants and a sporty gray lesbian T-shirt. I looked cute in that shirt, but forgot that I sweat in it. I was self-conscious the entire time, making sure that it didn't show through. The fibers in that shirt should be burned. What a girl will go through to look cute!

I was uncomfortable at first, but started fitting in as the room filled with over 70 lesbians. I was sitting on the couch, talking to a sweet woman, watching the game and having a grand old time, when suddenly Ms. Malibu walked into the room. Ugly as anticipated and attitude for days; I never really spoke to her except for "Hello" when Ms. Beverly Hills introduced us, and "Good-bye" when she left. I purposely never allowed myself to talk to her. Don't know why; just didn't. There was a weird tension that existed between the two of us.

It was finally time for me to leave. Before leaving, Ms. Beverly Hills pulled me aside and said, "I have to say thank you. I have been meaning to tell you that ever since meeting you, I now have faith that there are good lesbian women out there worth dating, and I never want to date a man. I don't know what I was thinking, but thank you."

I said "You're welcome and don't settle for less."

That was sweet. She is great, and rest assured I will be there next Super Bowl if I am invited! I left with no numbers in hand because I think that is tacky! I came home to an e-mail from Ms. Beverly Hills wanting to get together for drinks Friday.

In the meantime, Ms. Laguna Beach has been e-mailing, and there are the many e-mails that I continue to receive daily. I feel guilty because I don't respond or I respond nicely that I am seeing somebody; if somebody takes the time to write, I feel the need to respond. That's the nice Kristin, when I have the time.

I did receive an e-mail this morning that struck my fancy. However, she is 34, has never been with a woman, and is stressed in answering a personal ad. I responded with:

"it's funny how people have a such a bad perception about personal ads but it's okay to meet a stranger in a bar after having a few drinks, go out with them another time alone and that is thought of as normal! We live in a funny world."

15

I then told her:

> *"you spell trouble to me, I see red flags everywhere but I will be more than happy to e-mail and talk about whatever it is you want to talk about, 34 never dated a woman, but answering a woman seeking a woman ad at 11:20pm, meaning after a few drinks last night after searching the love at online lesbian dating ads you finally hit the send button and now thinking what the hell have I done! I understand, we have all been there before and it's frustrating!"*

She responded with lots of e-mails and photos, and clearly wants to start dating. I slowly withdrew myself from her life as she is not what I am looking for in a partner, and I don't have the time or energy to be her mentor lesbian!

To be honest, I am happy with Ms. New York. X-#2 saw me online last night, figured that I was back in town. She called me wanting to come over for sushi. I told her "No" as I am done with her; love her, but never again!

I'm practicing what I preach; that is, I'm starting to feel something with Ms. New York, so why taint it by going back to a dead relationship, no thank you! I'll give this a shot. I'm still open to meeting others, but with great caution, as we are not exclusively dating each other. Hell, we haven't even met in person! Who knows what will happen? But I am having a great time and I have met some lovely women and made new friends.

CHAPTER 7

The other day, I logged onto the Internet, went into my inbox, and who should I receive an e-mail from but Ms. Malibu. A little later than I had anticipated, but it did arrive. She is fed up with Internet dating. She was wondering if I had met anybody. If not, I should drop her a line; funny how that works. I have been waiting for that e-mail ever since the Super Bowl party. I just knew that she would e-mail me; the energy between us was negative but still there. I didn't respond for over a week, but finally gave in. I sent her a nice e-mail, since I am friends with Ms. Beverly Hills and they are friends; I don't want to burn any bridges. I told her that I was into a girl from New York, she wrote back stating that she had recently gotten back together with her ex-girlfriend. Lesbians seem to have a tough time with clean breakups; they tend to go back and forth several times with their exes before it is finally over.

Ms. Laguna Beach and I e-mail back and forth. She recently sent me an e-mail stating that she was going out of town for two weeks but would catch up when I returned from Paris, so we shall see what transpires, if anything.

Ms. New York and I are into each other. For my birthday, she sent me a silver bracelet from Tiffany's. I had never received a little blue box with a white ribbon. That scored her major points, as it was very romantic.

We have talked on the phone almost every night for the past six weeks. We enjoy talking, e-mailing and sending gifts to one another. She sent me more CDs that she made me. I sent her a package in return with CDs, a candle, and the vibrating egg. We talked about that one evening. She had never heard of it before; I couldn't resist, and lesbians sure do love their vibrators. She loved it.

I shortly left for Paris on business. She called me several times on my cell phone. It was a nice surprise. Calling internationally takes a lot of patience. I sent her a package that should have arrived today: a nice bottle of champagne (she is a champagne connoisseur, a.k.a. Kristin goes broke whenever I take her out to dinner in the future, add $100 to every bill), five more CDs (because she left the ones I previously sent her in a taxi), and another candle. Tonight she is sitting fifth row in a New York theater watching *Rent*. I was invited but couldn't attend because of work; hate that. She sure does have the life! She ended up going with her ex-girlfriend. Of course she did. Can one not see a pattern here in lesbian dating?

We are to meet in the Orlando airport shortly. She purchased her plane ticket. I have a copy to ensure that she had in fact booked her flight. We have our own rooms. She made the reservations. Adjoining rooms, as Sister said, "Is the most expensive insurance policy that I have." She booked a rental car, for which I insisted on a PT Cruiser. I know... cheesy. But I love the gangster car as a rental car. She doesn't know better, because she cabs it everywhere. She will hate me when she sees it, but I'll deal with that at that time. We will check in, get situated, and then I will take over. I asked her out on the date, so I have to knock on her door. We will go over to Pleasure Island to a nice restaurant. Then dancing at some heterosexual club, be hit on by men, then we will leave, and who knows what will happen, hopefully a great kiss at the door. We will go our separate ways, and only a wall will separate us. She will call. I will come over and we will end up in her bed cuddling for the evening. Then we will have massages at the spa in the morning. Drive to gay Florida for the day. Then home on Sunday.

That is my plan, and hopefully all goes well, because two weekends after that, we have talked about going snowboarding in Colorado. She has a condo in Steamboat Springs. She wants to teach me how to snowboard before all the snow melts. Then I will complete my two tournaments for work and hopefully spend one week in New York with her for my upcoming week's vacation.

Besides all of that fun, X-#2 has been freaking out lately. She has been e-mailing, calling, and continues showing up at my house at weird hours. She wants to get back together. I finally had to send her the dreaded "I love you but I'm not in love with you" e-mail, the "I'm seeing somebody else, move on" e-mail.

It didn't sit well. She fired back with three nasty e-mails that I never responded to. Hopefully I won't hear from her again. She told me she was dating somebody but ended things because she loved me and thought things could work out between us. I told her again that she shouldn't have ended things with the girl. I thought she was going to kill me, but she didn't. Thankfully I am still here writing.

Then one day, out of the blue, I received an e-mail from Ms. Lawyer. She sounds great; they all do! She used to be a professional tennis player until she broke her back. Then she became a lawyer, hated it, quit, and now sells real estate. Her father passed away several weeks ago. We have been e-mailing back and forth. Things are going along splendidly. We are to meet in the near future if we are ever in Los Angeles at the same time. She has been traveling a lot since the death of her father. She e-mailed me tonight, telling me that her cat passed away and how she just wants this month to end. She is going to visit her mother for a few weeks in Florida.

I like Ms. New York, but again how does an East Coast/West Coast relationship really work? And now there is a connection that is forming between Ms. Lawyer and me through our daily e-mails. Internet dating sure has been interesting, to say the least.

CHAPTER 8

I last left off with Ms. Lawyer going to Florida to be with her mother. Her mother is a Realtor in Sarasota. After numerous e-mails, we put together that my ex-mother-in-law is a Realtor in Sarasota, Florida as well. After having to explain that I once was married—not a fun topic for a lesbian—she went to a party and ran into my ex-mother-in-law! She sang my praises, and Ms. Lawyer immediately e-mailed me. She was excited to meet me in a few weeks. We exchanged phone numbers, which I won't use, but the gesture was sweet. We e-mailed about lesbian dating. She's dating and I am dating, so all is good—a conversation most lesbians don't normally have.

I finally met Ms. New York. I worked all week, then found myself sitting in an airport terminal in Florida, waiting for a stranger to show up. Fortunately I was too exhausted to be really nervous, but I was scared. I said good-bye to my co-workers then raced off to meet her. Her flight arrived early. I was anxiously searching for her, trying to be cool, but she had already seen me. She walked up to me; we hugged and said hello. She looked like her pictures, hoping I did too. We rented a car—they were out of PT Cruisers—and drove to the hotel. We got along well. We ended up having adjoining rooms, which was nice, but also scared me at first, as I like my space. We unpacked, then went to Pleasure Island. She had a water massage. I, of course, was too cool for that, plus it gave me 15 minutes to call Sister to give her an update.

We went to dinner and had champagne, stone crab claws, etc. We drank and ate and had great conversation. We ended up back at our rooms, with the door open, looking at each other. She said, "Let's watch a movie in my room."

I said, "Great."

We immediately ended up cuddling on her bed, watching *City of Angels*. It was comfortable and sweet. I was happy. She suddenly grabbed my hand and started asking questions about the lines in the palm of my hand. It was cute, but I wasn't going to give in, only because I was scared. But it felt good. She finally sat up and said, "Are you going to kiss me or what?"

I laughed and said, "Of course," and I kissed her. It was a sweet moment. It was all downhill from there. We ended up sleeping together the best that two drunken people can. The next morning, I awoke with a woman in my arms in a hotel room in Florida, with scheduled massages in a few hours. We woke up, did the uncomfortable kiss/touching thing as if it were a normal occurrence that we partook in; then we headed down to the spa.

We each had massages and then putzed around the spa. It was fun, but it was different. Being on a date with a lesbian lover in a naked spa is kind of odd. We had a moment when she wanted to wear her robe up to the room in her socks and tennis shoes. I immediately offered her my slip-on shoes. She said, "What are you going to wear?" I hemmed and hawed and finally she caught on and said, "You think I look stupid in these shoes?" I finally agreed. She finished tying the last string. She strutted out of the spa in her full glory, stopping in the gift shop, then continued to strut through the lobby and back up to the room. I was Shallow Hal for a moment. I tagged along smiling because she did look cute.

We spent the day in bed, drinking and watching movies, until I started freaking out on the inside. She may not have noticed at that moment. Then we went back to our favorite restaurant, where we had champagne and stone crab claws. Then we returned to her room. By the time we awoke in the morning, I was completely freaked out. It was all good, but I wasn't expecting any of this. My mind started messing with me. I was up at 4 a.m. walking around, antsy, not sure what to do. I crawled back in bed, woke her at 5 a.m. by mistake. She asked me what was wrong. I said nothing. I lay silently trying to fall back asleep, but I couldn't. Finally I did. She woke up, brushed her teeth, then came back to bed snuggling. It would have all been fine if I wasn't so freaked out on the inside. We finally got up and ordered room service. I, of course, couldn't eat. I jumped up, packed, and was ready to go!

She was confused, and I felt bad. I was clearly distant. It was all so weird for me; I felt completely removed on the inside. We checked out and drove to Church Street Station in Orlando. We had a nice lunch on a patio café, then dropped off the rental car. We were in different terminals. She rushed off to her security gate, not realizing that I wouldn't be allowed through; but I was okay with that. I gave her a quick good-bye hug and retreated back to my gate.

I came home to an apartment that had been half-looted by X-#2. She had convinced my pet sitter that it was okay for her to come in and remove her stuff. A few hours later, Ms. New York called and we talked on the phone. She called me on my behavior. She said that at first I was open and then I was aloof. I was. I was confused at this point. I liked her, but she lived in New York and I lived in Los Angeles, and something was missing. I couldn't put my finger on it, but something just wasn't there.

I immediately e-mailed Ms. Beverly Hills upon my arrival. She had told me about this girl, Ms. Comedian, who apparently liked me from the Super Bowl party. I ordered a date as soon as possible. She agreed. A group of us met the next evening. Ms. Comedian looked hot! When I met her Super Bowl weekend, she did not look hot! But she did this evening. I thought she was amazing. She thought I was amazing. I was overly confident. My friend had previously told me that she had slept with a girl whom she had met at her Super Bowl party; therefore, I had no worries in sharing my relationship dating experiences. She didn't care. She was into me.

She is a stand-up comedian in Los Angeles. She invited me to this lesbian event on an island in the Bahamas at the end of April during my week off. I, of course, agreed instantly but finally said that I wasn't sure, but would like to. She asked me if I had ended things with Ms. New York, and I said "No."

We all hung out, drank way too much, then dispersed one by one. It was a lot of fun and just what I needed. Ms. Comedian left for Japan today, but we are supposed to get together in one week.

Ms. New York was in Colorado with her brother, snow boarding, and we continued to talk every day. I liked her. We have agreed to meet at her condo in Colorado in a few weeks. Then she is flying to Las Vegas to meet me after my work tournament. Then I am going to New York to visit her, or to the lesbian island in the Bahamas, or to visit my friend in Portland, but I would prefer New York at this moment, to be honest! So there you have it, love at online lesbian dating is all good!

CHAPTER 9

I last left off with Ms. New York in Colorado, snowboarding with her brother. I am about to meet Ms. Lawyer within the next week or two, and I am going out with Ms. Comedian at the end of this week. It's a lot to keep up with, and let me say that all of them know about each other, so I am not doing anything deceptive; important to this kid. Adding in the numerous e-mails I receive daily, this really has been a trip!

Ms. New York was pretty much unavailable while on vacation, so I took up with others. I liked Ms. Comedian, but she was on the road in Japan. Ms. Lawyer and I continued our online relationship while she was in Florida with her mother. We agreed to meet in person when she was back in Los Angeles. However, she was busy so we were to play it by ear. No problem here, because I already had a date set up with Ms. Comedian this Thursday evening, and with our friend, Ms. Beverly Hills.

At last, Wednesday comes along. Ms. Lawyer is supposed to be booked all week, but decides at the last minute that she can fit me into her schedule. I told her that I was available last minute, as I kept my schedule open during the week after work in hopes of meeting her. I left work after her unexpected phone call, got home and had an hour to get ready. I decided to check my e-mail. While doing this, I received an I.M. from Ms. Beverly Hills confirming plans for Thursday evening with her and Ms. Comedian. I confirmed but was rushed. We bantered back and forth. She said that Ms. Comedian says hello. I told her to tell her hello, and that I thought she was cute. I hadn't realized that they were I.M.'ing me together, but I shortly caught on. They started asking a lot of questions regarding my relationship with Ms. New York and whether I was still chatting with her. I evaded the question by typing, "I can only I.M. one person at a time or I would have carpal tunnel syndrome."

Suddenly, Ms. New York saw me online and started I.M.'ing me. I hadn't heard much from her since she got back in town. She had gotten caught up with the drama of her ex, and then she had gotten sick. So I was surprised to hear from her, but she was back to her flirty fun self. She had obviously worked through her issues with her ex, and was back into me, go figure. Her timing couldn't have been worse. She was confirming the dates that she was coming to Los Angeles to visit me the following weekend.

I had 30 minutes until my date with Ms. Lawyer. I raced around getting ready, I.M.'ing both, when I received a third I.M. from Ms. New Orleans. I about had a heart attack. The first woman I ever answered an online ad to three years ago. She started I.M.'ing me. What a coincidence! Or was it? We never dated. She was too old and passed me on to X-#1. We became fast friends, but we hadn't talked since X- #1 and I broke up.

I started freaking out; this was all too weird. Then suddenly my computer died. I looked down. My friend's cats who were staying with me accidentally stepped on the power cord and disconnected everything! I was in shock, and I began laughing. I now had 20 minutes until my date with Ms. Lawyer.

I rebooted the computer, logged back online to see that Ms. New York and Ms. Beverly Hills/Ms. Comedian had logged off. I I.M.'ed Ms. New Orleans, explained what occurred, and ended that I.M. immediately. I sent the other two e-mails explaining what had happened. I was exhausted at this point. I finished getting ready and raced off to meet Ms. Lawyer.

I was a nervous wreck. I calmed myself down in the parking lot, and walked into Lola's Restaurant to meet Ms. Lawyer ten minutes late. This does not look good, but isn't bad, considering what I had just been through. I looked around and didn't see her. I scanned the bar again. This time I saw a striking girl at the bar, and realized that it was her. "Wow" is all that I said as I walked over to her. We hugged, said hello, and ordered drinks. We had an amazing time, and we got along splendidly, talking for hours, drinking way too much. Then somehow, I agreed to go back to her house. I don't know how, and I don't care why, but I was happy.

I followed her home, parked, and went inside. We decided that it was best if we both drank water. I walked around, looked at her cute apartment, and played with her adorable kitties. We listened to music and talked. Suddenly she walked up to me and started kissing me. It was a great moment; then she looked at me and said, "Were you ever going to kiss me?" I said "No." She laughed and said, "I could tell." We fooled around for a little bit and before I knew it, it was 2 a.m. I had to work in the morning. I liked her. She liked me. So I left and went home.

I was in heaven in my mind, walking down my hallway. I was replaying the events of the evening in my head, only to stumble across two boxes outside my front door with a note that read:

"Accidentally grabbed these, thought they were mine. Please leave my x-mas box outside your door. ~X-#2."

I was in shock. That crazy woman had the nerve to drop my stuff on my doorstep with me coming home after another amazing evening with a woman, only to make me feel as if X-#2 and I broke up again for the zillionth time! I suddenly became angry. I pulled my stuff inside the door, picked up the phone to call her, but decided not to. I sat down at my computer to e-mail her, but decided against that. That is when I found a sweet e-mail from Ms. Lawyer stating what a wonderful evening she had. I responded with a similar e-mail; it was clear that we were smitten with one another.

I decided to ignore X-#2. In fact, I never responded either way. I did e-mail Ms. New York about what had occurred, because we are tight about stuff like that and she is going through a similar thing. I got to vent and not do anything that I would regret! What a crazy evening, is all I can say!

I went to work to find that Ms. New York had purchased her tickets to come visit me in Los Angeles next weekend. I was happy, but now in a quandary. Again, they all know about each other, so I wasn't doing anything wrong. I wasn't expecting to like Ms. Lawyer, but I did. I e-mailed Ms. New York and told her that I was happy that she finally purchased her tickets, and we will have a fun weekend. I then realized that this evening I am supposed to meet Ms. Comedian. I don't want to anymore; lesbian West Hollywood is small enough. I don't need to add any more drama when I know that I am into another woman or two. I sent her a nice e-mail stating that I will try to make it this evening, but no promises.

Ms. Lawyer and I e-mailed back and forth all day, both giddy about our new mutual fondness for each other. She had plans. She canceled them and invited me to join her and her friends for dinner and drinks. I politely declined. I was exhausted and offered to meet up with her afterwards. She could come over to my house, since she would be in the neighborhood. After several e-mails, she finally said that she was "Slightly more than attracted to me," that she does not want to mess things up with us jumping into bed, and that it would be best if I met her out in a public place for a drink.

I agreed. I met her for a drink later that evening. She introduced me to her friends. She was clearly excited about introducing me to them as the new girl that she was into. I found it endearing. She certainly knew a plethora of lesbians at the bar, but was completely into me. It was cute.

There was a moment when she looked at me and said, "Do you know what I find hard not doing right now?"

Shy Kristin said, "Yes, but I'm not going to say." She was egging me on, but her friends were there and I wasn't going to say anything. At one point, a woman was in the middle of a lesbian drama breakup, asking for advice. Long story short, it spills out that Ms. Lawyer and she used to sleep together. Suddenly everybody looked at me. I said nothing. I nodded my head, trying to be cool, yet not surprised.

Ms. Lawyer immediately said, "Ah well, Kristin doesn't know that yet... ahh, we haven't gotten that far and I mean..."

Thankfully, her other friend cuts her off and says, "Honey, I think Kristin got that point, let's move on." I agreed. *Lesbian drama* is all that I was thinking at the moment. Later, we were all mingling and the friend looked at me and said, "All I can say to you is GOOD LUCK." We laughed and we went to another lesbian bar.

We had a good time. Finally, Ms. Lawyer said, "Do you remember the question that I asked you earlier?"

I said "Yes."

She said "Hands?"

I said, "I thought it was kissing but I understand."

She said "Is it okay? I don't know what the rules are."

I said, "I have no problem holding hands, touching in public, we are in a gay bar." She immediately grabbed my hand and started teasing me, but in a sweet way. She was putting herself out there in front of her friends with a new girl, and I liked that.

People started dispersing one by one, when she finally looked at me and said, "We can do one of two things: stay here with this boring lesbian crowd or go back to my house for 30 minutes of alone time."

I looked at her and said, "Let's go." Mind you, we had agreed earlier through our e-mail bantering that we would NOT sleep with each other because we both thought that this relationship was worth not being sabotaged by rushed sex and confusing false intimacy with real feelings.

Her friends had conveniently left, so I agreed to take her home. We drove to her house. We went inside her apartment, fooled around a little bit—not much, because we didn't want to "Break the rules." We had a great time. We laughed, talked, and cuddled. It was really sweet. I awoke at 6 a.m., as she didn't have an alarm clock. I was fearful of being late, but realized that I had plenty of time. We lay in bed, trying to behave ourselves, but certainly pushing the boundaries, when I finally had to pry myself away. I raced home, an hour late to work, but it was well worth it in my mind!

This evening is our scheduled date. We are both happy, giddy, excited. I left work and went home to shower and go over to her house. She was leaving on an early flight in the morning. We ordered food and hung out at her house while she packed. We finally nestled into the couch, agreeing to watch a movie and go to bed early. I would take her to the airport.

Again we are on our best behavior. No sex is going to happen; we want to get know each other better. She is out of town for the next ten days. We agreed that we may sleep together when she returns. Maybe not for another month or so, to make sure that it was right! We both clearly liked each other. We flipped through the channels and watched a movie called *40 Days and 40 Nights,* not realizing what the content was. We quickly discovered that it was a movie about a boy who gives up sex for Lent. We were watching him explain that when somebody says you can't have sex, that is all you think about. We laughed. She said, "Do you want to just have sex now?"

I laughed and said "No."

She said, "I know. I wasn't going to, but it was funny." We were both dying on the inside, but doing the right thing.

We finished the movie and went to bed, me in my clothes. I was actually comfortable, even though she didn't believe me; but I assured her I was, and I was. We snuggled and slept well. We got up early and I took her to the airport. We held hands the entire way, talked, laughed, etc. It was nice. We pulled up to curbside check-in. All eyes were on the car because of tightened security. I became uncomfortable with the lesbian good-bye kiss and hug, with all eyes watching us. She leaned over to kiss me and I gave her a hug. That was not very well received. She laughed and said "You are dissing me on the kiss, and give me a hug?"

I laughed and said "No, yes, but come on. I get shy sometimes, not always, but yes now." She understood, kind of, not really, so I gently grabbed her chin and gave her a kiss and a good-bye hug.

She perked up but said, "I'll have you know when I get out of this car, I'm going to scream and point - this is a lesbian driving this car."

I laughed and said "R i g h t." She grabbed her stuff and walked away. I am to see her in ten days.

As I drove home, happy with where things stood, suddenly my cell phone rang. It was Ms. Lawyer wanting to chat before she boarded her flight. She called me on my stuff. I said, "Call me when you get back in town on the 9th."

She was now laughing. She said "Yeah, call when I get back on the 9th, right; silly girl, you knew I would call you before that."

I said, "Yes, I was just saying that when you got back in town to call me."

She said, "Okay, silly." We had a good conversation and she was gone.

I went home, only to run into Sister, who informed me that X-#2 had been over the evening before, acting weird, looking for her Christmas box. For the love of getting out of my life. I was now mad, very mad. I sent her an e-mail saying that I would put her stupid Christmas box outside my door Monday, but that I was surprised somebody needed it eight months before Christmas! I didn't hear back, but her box was outside my door.

CHAPTER 10

I last left off with dropping Ms. Lawyer off at the airport for her departure for ten days, Ms. New York about to come to Los Angeles, me about to leave for another work tournament, and blowing off Ms. Comedian. Things were starting to get complicated, mixed up, not intentionally, but women don't usually juggle women, nor want to. But again, all of them know that I am dating!

Ms. New York and I started e-mailing and talking on the phone throughout the week. I told her that I was available Monday and Tuesday for talking on the phone, but after that, I was unavailable until Saturday! She knew I was supposed to meet Ms. Lawyer. She was guarded and distant. I sent her an e-mail explaining that I was insulted that she was coming to town and staying in a hotel, that I was fed up with her distance because of her issues with her ex, and that caused me to look elsewhere; that I met Ms. Lawyer. I liked her and I was now in a situation that I didn't ever expect to be in. I told her I was mad at her because she had the chance to tell me not to meet her or anybody else. But she didn't, and now we are where we are and not looking back!

She was hurt. I felt bad. We finally cleared everything up. She is still coming to Los Angeles next weekend and Las Vegas two weeks later. She ended her last e-mail by stating that I now had the pool of women to choose from that I always wanted; I hated her, but she was correct!

Ms. Lawyer started e-mailing and calling me daily. I set the record straight with her that I am not a phone person. She is. I am not, and Ms. New York and I have the phone and I don't have the need or energy to start that with another. Ms. Lawyer was not happy. She turned me on to text messaging and e-mail through my cell phone. I immediately called Nextel and got the feature turned on for $15.00 a month. I am a sucker for women. I took up and immensely enjoyed the text messaging and e-mail feature from my phone while on the road at my next tournament. Mind you, the rest of my crew is unhappy that I have suddenly become anti-social and disappeared into my cell phone! Ms. Lawyer and I send salacious e-mails back and forth throughout the week. She was hanging out with her lesbian tennis friends, watching tennis matches, e-mailing and text messaging me sexual e-mails while I was working and loving every minute of it.

In the meantime, Ms. New York and I started talking about real issues. She asked a lot of questions about Ms. Lawyer. I didn't give her much, just enough, because I didn't want her to torture herself. She was intrigued and hurt, and wanted to talk about our future. We normally talk about fun stuff—nothing sexual, just our lives. She had become my best lesbian friend, but then decided to try to take it to the next level. One night, she e-mailed me a sexual e-mail. We don't do that. I liked it, but I was surprised, and ever since, she had been open about wanting to date me and take this to the next level!

I was confused. Ms. Lawyer was on a roll text messaging me, e-mailing me, and calling me randomly. We were having a ball. There was one moment while I was in Las Vegas; I was laying on the bed while Sister was running around getting ready. I had just hung up the phone with Ms. New York. Ms. Lawyer text messaged me. While I was checking my e-mail, I received two online lesbian ad responses. I started laughing! Sister looked at me and said "What?"

I explained and we both laughed. I said "I swear I am not making this stuff up."

She said, "I know, only you." I didn't have the energy for all of this. It was fun at the moment, but feelings were starting to develop, and that was not cool.

Ms. Lawyer and I text messaged and e-mailed sexual messages throughout the week. Ms. New York and I talked on the phone, excited about our upcoming plans. In the meantime, I am working my ass off, but both would have no clue because they were both on vacation for the month!

I talked to Ms. New York on the phone and confirmed our plans to meet the following evening. She was excited. I was excited. I left Reno and came home. Upon my arrival, Ms. Lawyer had decided to get serious with me. We started e-mailing and then I.M.'ing again. She asked me what I thought about her when I first met her. We both exchanged war stories. She hinted that she had mailed me something which would arrive at my house while Ms. New York is here tomorrow. Lovely, is all I can say! Ms. Lawyer then officially asked me out on a date for the 11th. Thank goodness it was only the 4th; so I was not doing anything wrong, right?

I am picking her up on the 9th from the airport with her new kitty that she just purchased. I told Ms. Lawyer that I had a friend in town for the weekend. She never said anything, as she was into her friends at the moment. Long story short: after two hours of I.M.'ing, Ms. Lawyer and I agreed that we have something special. The phone rang; it was Ms. New York calling from Arizona on a business conference; I didn't answer. I felt guilty, but should I? Yes I should and I do, but I really shouldn't because I hadn't done anything wrong. I had only met Ms. New York in person once. I had only hung out with Ms. Lawyer three evenings. Ms. Lawyer and I ended our I.M. We were set for the 9th for me to pick her and her kitty up from the airport.

Ms. New York called back. I answered the phone and we talked for quite some time. We were both excited that we will spend the weekend together, that this will be the second time that we have actually seen each other. She happened to be spending the evening in the honeymoon suite of some hotel in Arizona and wished that I were there. She can't wait to be here this weekend. I agreed.

Ms. New York arrives tomorrow to spend the weekend with me. Ms. Lawyer is lingering in my head, and I feel that I am doing something wrong, but I am not. I know I sound like such a tramp, but I am not. I have only slept with four women, not something either one of them can say.

Ms. New York and I will have a great weekend. Ms. Lawyer wanted to start talking more on the phone, but I have told her no; I want her in person, not on the phone. I hope she doesn't start calling this weekend, but I have a feeling she will.   I don't know what to do about the text messaging, other than put my phone on vibrate, tell her that my friend is in town, and that I am busy. She understands, as she is busy with her friends at the moment!

Then Ms. New York leaves on Monday. I pick Ms. Lawyer up on Wednesday evening and we are supposed to "sleep together." I mean that in the sense of only sleeping and kissing and no more, because we have a real date on Friday evening. That is the night that we will sleep together! Then I leave the following Wednesday for Las Vegas. Ms. New York is flying out to spend Easter weekend with me in Las Vegas, which I am looking forward to. Fortunately, Ms. Lawyer will be in Florida visiting her mother, so all is good on that end! Then things get tricky the following week. I have a week's vacation, for which I have three options. Ms. New York is pressuring me to visit her, to which I had agreed, taken back, agreed, taken back, and finally said that we will discuss it this weekend! What can a girl do? Ms. Lawyer knew I was supposed to go to New York; she asked me and I told her that I wasn't going, because at that time, I wasn't. She never asked any more questions. I will more than likely stay home, because by then, they will both want a marriage commitment!

I was talking to Ms. New York this evening, and she started asking more questions about Ms. Lawyer. I love her for being honest, but I chose not to answer. I think she is now more interested in me because somebody else is interested. She asked about my book and asked if Ms. Lawyer was in these last two chapters, because I refused to read them to her. She is a smart girl. She laughed and said "I don't care. I will have you in your bed tomorrow evening and that's all that matters." In her mind, she was correct.

As much fun as all of this sounds, it really is not. Feelings have developed and I will need to make a choice in the next few weeks. If I were to guess right now, I would pick Ms. Lawyer. There is something between Ms. Lawyer and me. I cannot explain what it is, but something is there. Maybe this weekend, with Ms. New York, she will give me something that is more than something local. I'm not sure.

Ms. New York arrives tomorrow. We will have a fun weekend. Ms. Lawyer will be lingering in the back of my head. As for the other e-mails that I receive daily, I don't dare answer them, nor do I want to; my hands are full!

CHAPTER 11

I last left off with Ms. New York coming to Los Angeles. She arrived. I had our driver pick her up and bring her back to my place. She walked through the front door. We hugged. She said that she was nervous. I wasn't, because it was my house. We had a few drinks, walked Lady, met Sister and her boyfriend, and then we hung out. We awoke in the morning and putzed around. She was sick from my friend's cats that were staying here, as she was deathly allergic to them.

We went to lunch, then we went to The Abbey. We met her friends and my friends, danced, drank, and had a great time. Then we went home and passed out. She left the next morning. I went to work to find a dozen roses from Ms. New York. Ms. Lawyer called a few times. She was busy with her friends and not really interested in what I was doing. It worked for that moment. We started e-mailing again and we were both looking forward to seeing each other.

I liked Ms. Lawyer and I knew it, hence the pit in my stomach and visions of her in my head ever since she left town. She was coming home in two days and I knew that I needed to end things immediately with Ms. New York. A few days passed. I called Ms. New York, leaving her several messages as we played phone tag. My time was coming to an end, so I ended up sending her an e-mail ending things.

I hated doing that, but knew it was the right thing to do for my future. She was upset. I was upset, but still knew it was the right thing to do. I told Ms. New York that she can't come to Las Vegas because I am into Ms. Lawyer and I didn't want to jeopardize anything with her. I canceled my upcoming vacation to New York because that wasn't right either. Lesbian drama. I had become exactly what I never wanted to become!

I then sent Ms. Lawyer an e-mail explaining that I had ended things with Ms. New York. Apparently, Ms. Lawyer doesn't read everything that I e-mail her, as she was surprised that I ended things with Ms. New York. She responded with an e-mail saying that she doesn't recall me dating her, but that she was happy that the relationship had ended.

I picked up Ms. Lawyer and the kitty from the airport Wednesday evening and we went back to her house. We all got settled and then crashed for the evening. We hung out the next morning, and I went to work. We were to have our second official date Friday evening. Well, it will actually be our first, because the first ended up being pizza on the couch. She surprised me and took me to this romantic restaurant, The Little Door. We had an amazing time. She looked incredible, better than any dish on the menu. We went back to her place, crashed, and spent the weekend together, before I headed out of town for work. We fooled around but never had sex. One day soon, but not quite yet. She needed to feel more comfortable with me before she trusted me fully, and I was okay with that.

CHAPTER 12

I arrived back in town Easter Sunday, anxious to see Ms. Lawyer. She was at her friend's house, but we were to meet up at my sister's house for dinner later in the afternoon. I was excited to see her. She finally called. I went to pick her up to bring her back to my sister's, for her to finally meet my friends. I drove over to her place, and walked into her apartment, only to find my smiling, cute, sweet Ms. Lawyer waiting for me. It was a great moment, to say the least, and long overdue. We hugged and we kissed. We went over to Sister's house for Easter dinner.

We had a great time, but I was anxious to leave, because I only wanted to be with her. We excused ourselves early. I, of course fell down a flight of stairs, cutting my hand, bruising my knee, and leaving me with a bruised ego but still happy. She was gracious and only laughed after knowing that I was not really hurt. We went back to my apartment and that was the evening that we had sex for the first time. It was a great moment; we were on her terms and it was a trusting experience for both of us. We left shortly afterwards and went back to her house, as she has a kitty that needs lots of love and attention.

I was falling for her and she for me. We spent the week working and seeing each other in the evenings. We joined her friends for drinks one evening, which started out as a lovely evening, only to end with one of the girls describing for 30 minutes the first time that she and Ms. Lawyer were intimate. It was something I didn't need to hear nor found amusing, but the girl clearly wanted to share, God knows why. Needless to say, it caused our first fight. I didn't blame Ms. Lawyer for the other girl's actions, but for the mere fact that she didn't ask her to shut her trap.

We left. I was finally able to breathe and to digest what had just occurred. To see nameless faces others have slept with is one thing, but once the person is there describing their intimate moments, it changes things. It just is that way and you either like them or you don't like them, and I definitely did not like this woman! We walked to the car and I drove Ms. Lawyer home. I went to drop her off at her house. She looked at me, confused, as I have never dropped her off without coming in before. I said, "I think it's best that I go home this evening." She disagreed. We got into it. I wasn't clear on what I was feeling, so I shut down. She was not happy; after a few tears and a little bit of back and forth, I went inside. She showered and we went to bed. I left early and we both felt weird.

I went to San Diego the next day for work. We e-mailed back and forth. Fortunately we were able to talk about why I was upset. She felt bad. I had been jealous and hurt without wanting to be. We worked through it, as I was to be at her house at 6:30. She was having a dinner party at seven for me to meet her other four friends. I didn't want to go, because she and I were off, but I ended up going over early. We talked through it and we ended up having a great evening. Of course, one of the four girls, she had slept with previously. I just felt it. She confirmed it later, but it didn't matter, because it was never thrown in my face like the previous encounter. It was all good and we survived our first fight!

We hung out Friday evening. Sometime during the week, we agreed that we were dating exclusively. We wanted to live together, as she had just bought a new condo. She is moving in several months. The plan is for me to move in with her in one year, so as to not be premature and not to mess things up. Lesbians tend to do that, but not us. She has never lived with anybody before, so we will take things slowly.

She was to leave town Saturday morning for one week, to go back to her hometown, go through her father's estate, and put their house on the market. I drove her to the airport early Saturday morning. I wasn't going to make the same mistake twice; I gave her a big body hug and kiss on the curb at the airport. I really wasn't trying to make up for last time; I just couldn't take my hands off of her. Funny what falling for a girl can do to a person.

CHAPTER 13

Internet dating is a hoot, to say the least, and the most amazing tool out there for people to meet other people. I received lots of e-mails from women every day, and I think it's about time that I shared with the world exactly what these e-mails contain. So here are a few of the e-mails that I have received and continue to receive every day:

"I am interested in talking with you. I am in Orange County...completing nursing school. I work as a veterinary technician and love it. I am feminine with reddish blonde hair. Love to play tennis and do anything athletic. Don't party though. So, e-mail me if you want. I will be waiting. 27lon"

"I'm not sure what a lawn shouter is - I do know that I like who I am - physically, spiritually, emotionally and my mind amuses me. I'm open to meet. I have a house in the mountains an hour and a half from LA - stars, quiet, flowers, streams, waterfall - and I'm in LA quite often. If you're interested I can send a picture. Will be in LA on Wed and Thurs. Take Care. Wahoot"

"Hello Lbspin, I saw your profile and thought we might get along great. My profile doesn't mention my athleticism since the extreme sport I endeavor in seems to intimidate people. I usually don't mention it much until someone gets to know me or in this case you mentioned you are also interested in an athletic person. Well, please check out my profile and let me know if you are interested. Sincerely, Bunny"

"I rarely e-mail, my profile is up but I don't check the site too often. I liked your profile and your look. Drop me a line. Aleeeeeh." (I e-mailed her back and told her that I was dating somebody.) Her response was *"She is a Lucky girl. You are down right gorgeous. Have a beautiful and romantic time together. How long have you been dating? Keep in touch. Aleeeeeh"*

"wanted to get back in touch with you. life got crazeeeeeeeeeee right b4 you went a cruisin' early march. will you still talk to me? (big smile, small voice!);) changed jobs - the competition recruited me, so i was traveling back east. left a company after 5 1/2 years that i was passionate about, had friends that were like family at, potty training dogs, you know—then again maybe you don't. how

37

are you? how are things? poker? dog? look forward to hearing from you." (Ms. Laguna Beach)

"i wanted everyone to find me except you... just to tease you.;)" (Ms. New York)

"I have long auburn hair, in good shape & financially secure. I take pride in my appearance & have been told by many that it shows. I love being outdoors, the beach, & going to nice places. I would love to share some good times with another beautiful & sexy woman who takes pride in her appearance. My picture is available to those who show a genuine interest! Runner"

"I thought that first quote was so funny. I am a first timer here tonight and I was just curious. I think what you wrote was funny. I don't have a picture yet, not too high tech with the dig. camera just yet. I am cute though and fem. I don't know if you can see my profile, but it tells all. If you want to talk e-mail me back. If it doesn't let you reply, write me at _____. Thanks (name)...why did I say thanks? Just envious I guess. Integrity"

"I haven't gone on this damn thing in months so I'm thinking if you haven't either, maybe you gave up on (love at online lesbian dating) or you already met your match but I thought I'd drop you a line anyway. If you're interested, e-mail me back!" (Ms. Malibu)

"Hello, I saw your profile and was very interested. I wanted take a chance on this website to meet a sweet normal woman. I've never done this sort thing before and are a private person, so please excuse the vague profile. So...if you are interested/available to meet a very nice woman, I look forward to hearing from you and I could tell you more about myself. Swtcalif"

"Hi, I am a new member and ran across your picture. You look like someone I might want to meet. They haven't posted my picture yet, but I hope they do soon. I know for you it must be difficult communicating with someone who you have no idea what they look like. Right now it is kinda one sided; I know what you look like, but you haven't a clue as to what I look like. I think you'll be happy once you see my picture. I am in the L.A. area all the time. Maybe we can meet one of these days. I hope to hear from you soon. 40and"

There you have a little insight into the joys of online dating. Hopefully it didn't go unnoticed that some of the responses have recently been from past correspondences. Ms. Laguna Beach resurfaced recently, as did Ms. Malibu. Ms. New York posted her own ad after our breakup, and she is doing well with love at online lesbian dating!

I have a new e-mail pursuer, Ms. Sake. We met through work. She recently found out that I was a lesbian and she has been pursuing me ever since. She sent me a "message in a bottle"—literally a message in a bottle asking me out to dinner; it was quite cute. I have always been intrigued with Ms. Sake. Neither of us knew that the other was definitely gay until recently in an e-mail I told her about my dinner date with Ms. Lawyer. Unfortunately, our timing was off. I informed her of my newly committed relationship with Ms. Lawyer. She took it quite well and we continue our friendship through daily e-mails and occasional work functions.

CHAPTER 14

Ms. Lawyer was back home with her mother, doing family things, and I missed her terribly. I was staying at her place. We joked that she would never get her house key back, because that is how lesbians operate. I was taking care of the kitties and writing this book. I sat down to write, when suddenly I received an e-mail. Something told me that it was from X-#2, whom I hadn't heard from in months, and sure enough it was. I opened the e-mail and this is what it said:

> *"hey, I hate to bother you but I was expecting a package. Unfortunately, since I am on my third address in less than six months... I am finally trying to get all my stuff to me, and some people still have your address and my previous one on ——. It takes time for these things to get situated. I was expecting a package a week or so ago...and I have checked my old address and it has not come there...it is very important. I wasn't sure if you were tossing any mail of mine or not... but I would appreciate it if you would set it aside. I realize that this is not your top priority. thanks... X-#2"*

I responded to her e-mail with the following:

> *"it's weird because i just heard the click for the e-mail and i knew it was from you... can't explain, just weird... i would never throw any of your mail away and no i haven't seen anything for you... i did get a message on friday from your bank about signing something, was going to call you or e-mail you but you delete everything, so i didn't...nothing has arrived but if it does i will tell you...*
>
> *congrats on _____!!! it's a huge success, good for you...i hear you have a new girl, congrats as well, i finally found one too!!!...very happy but working and traveling way too much, girls don't like that but hopefully this one will... i will let you know if i receive anything but nothing yet! bye, Kristin"*

Apparently, whatever I wrote set her off like a time bomb. I was writing and I.M.'ing Ms. New York when X-#2 started I.M.'ing me, asking me:

> *"why do you have to bring up anything other than the mail?"*

I apologized. For what, I don't know, but I did, and then she wrote:

> *"i had written you a letter ...but never sent it...you were mean to me a lot...it took me 12 weeks of intensive therapy for my therapist to admit that things were not all me...and that you have issues...i protected you and put you on a pedestal for so long......never acknowledging how shitty you were"*

The I.M. went downhill from there. Next thing I knew, my cell phone was ringing, and I responded via I.M. that I was not taking her phone calls, that again I was sorry for how things ended. Can we just put the past behind us and move forward? She continued to rant and rave. Finally I had to literally turn the computer off in order to stop her from I.M.'ing me. I turned my phone off too. Drama is all that I can say in regard to lesbian dating sometimes.

I e-mailed her the next day, apologizing because I recognized that she was hurt and was coming from a bad place. She deleted the e-mail without reading it. Several weeks later, I received the following e-mail from her:

> *"hey, sorry to keep bugging you...but hopefully over the next five years i will have all my personal belongings back. I think you may have that little picture of me as a baby, the one that you hated and ask me to put away. That is my only copy...it should be easy to depart with... can you let me know...X- #2"*

I responded with:

> *"i don't hate that photo and yes i'm sure i still have it in the drawer where it was last left...when i go home this evening i will look for it, where would you like me to leave it?...would you like me to forward you the uta list or do you have a source in obtaining that?...i saw you the other day at the coffee bean while i was on my way to the airport...i hope all is well and let me know what you would like me to do with the photo...kristin"*

She responded with:

> *"well kristin, that is about the nicest response that i have gotten from me in a long time...i never know with you if you will be in attack mode or what... just let me know if you have that pic and i can swing by and pick it up... by the way do you have the extensions to my vacuum...i know that is a silly request...but you*

wouldn't believe how my back hurts when i have to bend down to the floor if you have that as well put in the usual pile by the door...thank you so much...X.-#2"

I responded with:

"X-#2, i will look for the vacuum extensions but i don't think so but i haven't looked either...i'll leave everything outside my door this evening after work...i'm not in attack mode, so no worries there...have a good day, Kristin"

She responded with:

"thank you...you have a good day too"

Later in the day, before I left work, I sent her the following e-mail:

"hey, i won't be going home this evening, so i will put your stuff out thursday evening...i didn't want you to waste your time but i'm sure everything is there...take care, Kristin"

Next thing I knew, my cell phone started ringing. I didn't pick up. She then called my work. I told the secretary to have her call my cell phone and I would pick up this time. She called me and started in with, why do I have to be so mean, and I had sent her that last e-mail so she would know that I was staying at my girlfriend's house that evening, and I was passive-aggressive! I explained that I'm sorry she felt that way. That is not true. I had told her about my girlfriend many weeks ago, and I was actually being polite, in that I didn't want her to waste her time going to my house when nothing would be there. She didn't believe me. I finally ended the conversation. For the love of trying to end a relationship!

CHAPTER 15

Things with Ms. Lawyer were going along, as my therapist said, "As planned." Not so sure that I liked that statement. We were three months into our relationship, the honeymoon phase was definitely over, and we were now entering into the first stages of a "real relationship." Not very happy here! I liked the honeymoon phase much better.

She was currently in Amsterdam for the next three weeks on vacation, while I was here in Los Angeles, pondering our relationship. The past four weeks had been tense, with both of us needing our space and distance. This was not a good sign for such a young relationship.

I continued to receive e-mails daily from interesting women, one of which I wanted to go out with; but I informed her of my relationship with Ms. Lawyer, so that was not an option. Last week, I unexpectedly received a business trip to Atlantic City. I went to New York for a few days prior to my work engagement, and stayed with Ms. New York. We were only friends, since we both have girlfriends. She was an excellent tour guide. She showed me New York City and we had a wonderful time before I rented a car and drove to Atlantic City. After that trip, I returned to Los Angeles to spend a few hours with Ms. Lawyer before I took her to the airport for her three-week vacation.

After she left, Ms. New York informed me that she was coming to Los Angeles for a work engagement that happened to fall during our gay pride. I was excited to have her here, as I love pride, and she asked if she could stay with me. At first I said yes, but then realized that it wouldn't be appropriate, so I told her that she needed to stay in a hotel. She was bummed, but she understood. She was also trying to get me to go to Paris with her five days prior to my upcoming Paris business trip. As much fun as that would be, I didn't think Ms. Lawyer would find that amusing in any way, so I declined out of respect for our relationship.

That said, I was catching a red-eye out on Friday the 13th with my sister, when I received an e-mail from Ms. Sake. She was bummed, having a bad day, and wishing that somebody would take her mind away from her stress for a few hours. So I anted up, (as we are both in the poker/casino business) and I told her that I was available from 8 p.m. to 11 p.m. if she wanted to come over to my house for drinks and Scrabble. She unexpectedly took me up on the offer, and I was pleasantly surprised, since I had just seen her several days earlier at a work function.

She drove up from Long Beach. We hung out for the first time one-on-one and we had a great time. She is older, wiser, and very kind. She brought me my favorite dessert, orange sherbet with sprinkles on the side, and doggie treats for Lady. That was very sweet and thoughtful of her. We sat around listening to music, talking, and enjoying each other's company. I read her several chapters of this book. She was intrigued, and before we knew it, Sister was knocking on the door for a ride to the airport. I walked Ms. Sake to her car, thanked her for a lovely evening, and said good night. Then Sister and I raced off to the airport; it was a splendid evening.

Throughout the weekend, I received a few text messages from Ms. Lawyer. She apparently has issues about not calling while away. I don't like this, but I needed to respect this about her. I just wished that she had informed me of this behavior before she hit foreign soil. I continued to e-mail Ms. New York and Ms. Sake daily, and Ms. Lawyer whenever she had time for it.

Ms. Sake sensed the ending of my relationship with Ms. Lawyer. She informed me in an e-mail this evening that she planned on changing her name in the book as she has earned this name by a fateful evening of mixing sake and wine while learning how to make sushi with some friends. The end result was missing the Long Beach Gay Pride Festival due to a major hangover. She told me that she plans on being the last chapter, that she is working on the content right now. One has to love her enthusiasm! I believe Ms. New York has the same intentions.

X-#2 e-mailed me yesterday, wanting nothing but to say hello. She was home sick and wanted to talk to a friend. I was pleasantly surprised that she wasn't mad at me for the first time, and that she didn't want anything from me. Then today I received another e-mail from her, asking if she could e-mail me some photos of her surfing and playing soccer. I agreed. Then she asked me out to lunch and I told her that I was no longer taking lunch breaks at work because I was too busy. We e-mailed back and forth a bit. It was nice, yet I sensed something odd; can't put my finger on it yet, but nice is good at the moment.

This coming weekend is gay pride, during which Ms. New York will be staying in a hotel nearby, Ms. Sake is coming up for the weekend, X-#2 will be out of town, X-#1 will join the rest of us for an interesting pride weekend, and Ms. Lawyer has now moved on to her other social events in London. The more the merrier!

An interesting lesbian experience lies ahead for this kid. I'm not into Ms. Lawyer anymore. She's not into me. Our relationship is definitely almost over. We have never spoken the words because we haven't been in the same city at the same time to break up, so at the moment we were still together. There is nothing wrong with hanging out with friends; she was doing the same thing at the moment, just on the other side of the world.

There were no coincidences in life, everything was meant to happen for a reason!

CHAPTER 16

"Wow" is all I can say at the moment. I will start off by saying exes cannot just be friends. Love at online lesbian dating was about to hit Los Angeles Gay Pride weekend to the fullest.

Ms. New York arrived, got settled into her hotel, and wanted to go out. I picked up X-#1 and the three of us hit gay Los Angeles! We started out in a trendy nightclub, only to miss Justin Timberlake and Christina Aguilera's after-hours party. Although we were invited, we chose to go to The Factory, the lesbian bar in town that has over 500 women. Boy, did we all have a great evening—dancing, drinking, great conversation, going on and on until the wee hours of the morning. We dropped X-#1 off and called it a night.

The next afternoon, the party started again. We met X-#1's friends at Here Bar. We were mingling, talking, and having great conversation when I noticed a girl across the bar. She looked like a professional volleyball player, and as it turned out she was. I was the only one of our group who thought she was cute. I kept trying to convince the others that she was cute. By the end of the evening, everybody thought she was hot, but she only had eyes for me. Flirting was fun. I was having a good time. Even though I have a girlfriend, there's nothing wrong with looking.

As the evening progressed and the alcohol started flowing, the lesbian drama started happening among the others, so we left to go dancing at another bar. On the way to the bar, Ms. Volleyball Player was walking by with her friends. We were walking by, and I was holding X#-1's hand, to keep her from falling. Ms. Volleyball Player yelled, "Hey, Kristin" and waved. I waved back with the hand that was holding X-#1's hand. I was cursing myself later for that dumb move, but it was innocent, so I didn't care. We had a great time, dancing, laughing; it was a great release. Ms. New York and I left shortly after, as X-#1 was meeting a date. I dropped Ms. New York off at her hotel room and went home alone.

The next day was Pride in Los Angeles. Ms. New York was tired and needed to rest, so X-#1 and I hit the parade early. We drank way too much, had way too much fun, met friends. Finally, Ms. New York joined us later in the afternoon. By this time, we were drunk. She was stone sober and found little humor in the two of us.

We ran into Ms. Sake and her friend along the parade route. We were going one way, they were going another. We said hello and goodbye, hoping to meet up at the festival later in the afternoon. We ended up not making it to the festival. We never left the bar, as we could barely move by the end of the afternoon, thanks to the many Red Bulls and vodkas that we consumed. But we were sure having a great time. We met up with a group of friends. We were having fun; the next thing I know, X-#1 started kissing me and I didn't stop her! Ms. New York flew off the handle because she knew that I would never cheat on my girlfriend, much less with X-#1. It was all in good fun, but Ms. New York was not amused. She got mad and the drama started. Finally X-#1 and I left the bar in a drunken stupor; we went back to her house and watched some of *The World Poker Tour*, and said goodnight. What an event, to say the least, but all pride festivals end with some kind of lesbian drama, that's a given!

I woke to messages from Ms. New York, who was leaving this day, mad at me. She left and I was left with the guilt of kissing X-#1 while my girlfriend was on vacation in London. This was not a good feeling and not something that I normally partook in. Again, my girlfriend and I weren't really communicating, as she refused to talk to me on the phone. Our e-mails had dwindled down to almost nothing and we rarely text messaged, every so often but not that much. Needless to say, as the days and weeks went by, we became more distant and un-communicative.

Several days before she was to return home, she e-mailed me, informing me that she had extended her stay one week. She also informed me that upon her return, she was spending the 4th of July with friends in San Diego. I leave for Paris a few days after the 4th of July.

I finally couldn't take any more of this. I sent her an e-mail ending our relationship. It was impossible to have a meaningful relationship with her, since she was always on the go. There was little, if any, real communication, and my needs weren't being met in many areas. She replied in an e-mail that she was distracted in her life and that she concurred in our relationship being over.

Wounded, yet understanding that she was not the one for me, I picked up the pieces. Fortunately I kept my ad on love at online lesbian dating and I had lots of offers. But I was in need of some immediate attention. I remembered the intrigue that I had always had with Ms. Sake. I e-mailed Ms. Sake, talked to her about what was going on, and before I knew it, we had a date to go to San Diego's Gay Pride Festival the following weekend.

Ms. New York was not speaking to me; X-#1 was just a friend, and Ms. Sake and I picked up where we last left off. I picked her up on Sunday at her house. We drove several hours to San Diego. We finally found parking. We were cursing the event planners for not having any signs up. We got on the trolley that the website told us about, toured around Balboa Park for 30 minutes, and found no festival!

We started acting stereotypical, looking for gay people to ask. Found none. We went to the Visitors' Center and they were clueless. We walked to a nearby grassy area, sat down, and started calling local gay bars that we knew of. They were closed because it was the middle of the afternoon. I finally called a friend to look up the Web site again, only to discover that we were one month early!

This was actually very funny! I have never felt more stupid. The only saving grace I had was that I had forwarded the Web site to Ms. Sake's e-mail address prior to our departure. So she was partially responsible, although she never looked at the Web site. But it made me feel a little better; not really, but kind of.

Thankfully, she was easygoing with a great sense of humor. She was able to see the humor in what we just experienced, or so I hoped. Either way she now had something to hold over my head for the rest of my life. That she definitely saw the value in! We left for Seaport Village to have a nice lunch and enjoy each other's company.

After the San Diego "non-Pride Festival" lunch and a stroll through Seaport Village, we drove back to Long Beach. We hung out at her house, laughed, and watched *Sex and the City.* Finally, it was time for me to leave. As I was leaving, she handed me a gift that she had purchased earlier in the day: the new Harry Potter book and a card. I thanked her and drove home. Once I arrived at home, I read the card. It was very sweet, saying what a great day she had "sans the festival!" I chuckled out loud, knowing that I will never live this one down!

CHAPTER 17

Here we are, the 4th of July weekend. I last left off with my relationship with Ms. Lawyer over, Ms. New York not speaking to me, Ms. Volleyball Player back in Arizona, X-#1 just a friend, and Ms. Sake and I ending a great San Diego non-Pride event. There is so much to tell, plus the endless online e-mails, so my life continues...

Ms. Lawyer and I were through. She was due home this evening from her one-month vacation in Europe. I was officially no longer her Sherpa. My duties were completed this morning. It was difficult saying good-bye to her kitties, until the kitten ran out the front door and sprinted down the hallway with no fear. Just my luck—the last feeding and I lose one. I sprinted after him, grabbed him just as he was about to turn the corner down the stairs, put him inside, locked the door, slid the key under the door, and left.

With that chapter closed in my life, my new life beckons. I had a date with Ms. Sake this Sunday. I had no clue what it was, as I had relinquished all control to her. We shall see what transpires; I am on a need-to-know basis, and all I know at this moment is that we have plans Sunday.

We were I.M.'ing last evening, downloading music, and having a good time, when my phone rang. I let the voice-mail pick up. After completing our I.M., I listened to the message. I was pleasantly surprised by a message from X-#1, at the lesbian bar, who happened to run into Ms. Volleyball Player. She left me a nice message saying that she was in town until Monday, wished I were there, and left her telephone number. I was thrilled because when I last met her, I had a girlfriend and never got her phone number. I called her back and left a message. We're going to try to get together sometime this weekend. If not, there will always be another time.

Today was the 4th of July, the only day that I could sneak into the office and actually get anything done before our Paris trip in three days. After completing some work, I returned home. I received a phone call from Ms. New York wanting to talk about "the weekend." For the love of wanting to relax! But I had put her off too long and I was thankful that she still wanted to have a friendship, so I took my beating. It was not pretty, but it was well-deserved. I listened and I got what she had to say. Fortunately she got sidetracked with another phone call, and we ended our conversation; but we will pick up at a later date. While talking to Ms. New York, she had me look up some women on love at online lesbian dating. I did, and here it goes again. I found some interesting women. I didn't respond to any of them because I was exhausted, but there were a few I think I may respond to in the morning.

Maybe I needed a break before I started over again, maybe not. Tomorrow I will see Ms. Volleyball Player and Sunday is Ms. Sake. Ms. Lawyer wanted to see me. We have been text messaging again, but I will not entertain that thought. Who knows how this weekend will unfold? It is only Friday on this three-day holiday weekend!

Saturday morning, I awoke to a 6 a.m. text message. Nobody text messages me except Ms. Lawyer. I woke up, rolled over, grabbed the phone and responded. But this time it wasn't Ms. Lawyer. It was Ms. Sake. I got busted so big time it wasn't even funny. Thankfully, I had been nothing but honest, but it wasn't pretty. Since Ms. Sake and I had been downloading music the evening before, I.M.'ing back and forth, she sent me a text message saying "A great makeout song is by Michael Jackson, Butterflies, download it, nite."

Apparently, she'd sent it at 11:30 p.m. but I didn't receive it until 6:00 a.m. I responded with, "I know. Are you on sitting on the airplane?" Okay, I couldn't get out of it, even if I tried, as she knew Ms. Lawyer was coming home today on an airplane from London, so I was screwed. After I sent the text message, I started wondering why Ms. Lawyer would make reference to making out. I then saw the phone number. "Ahhh," I gasped, wondering what do I do now.

I sent another text message immediately saying "Good morning, I hope this wakes you early on the 4th, as yours just came through." Then I got up and sent her an e-mail with the following:

"thanks a lot for waking me up at the crack of dawn!!!...i did awake to a text message at the crack of dawn, nobody text messages me but ms. lawyer, so i thought she was bored sitting on the airplane listening to michael jackson, she text messaged me not caring what time it was for me...after i responded i thought that was odd that she would write what a great make out song...i reread the message to discover that it was from you and that you sent that and that made much more sense...then i text messaged you back hoping that i was able to return the favor of waking you up at the crack of dawn on the 4th of july...today i have learned another lesson and

50

that is to check the phone number of the text messenger before responding...how many lessons do i get to learn this week?..."

I hadn't heard from Ms. Sake; she was out for the 4th of July. But I did receive a few text messages from Ms. Lawyer, one actually asking when I was leaving for Paris. Interesting, but I have no intentions of seeing her before I leave.

CHAPTER 18

I woke to e-mails from Ms. New York apologizing to me for having to take another phone call as she was about to leave for her European vacation; Ms. Sake not mad at me, actually not mentioning the text message. Ms. Volleyball Player and I exchanged several phone calls throughout the day, leaving me to call her before I left for Paris the next day. Ms. Lawyer, back in town, exchanged a few nice short e-mails.

Ms. Sake and I had plans Sunday. Lady and I drove to her house. She had a cooler packed with water and sodas, and we headed off to the dog beach in Huntington Beach. We had a fabulous time, mainly with me carrying Lady the entire time. She played in the water with a few other dogs as we sat on a blanket, laughing and talking the day away. We spent far too much time in the sun, then walked back to her car, where we found a parking ticket. We headed to Second Street and had dinner at a nearby café that allowed dogs. We hung out for a few hours conversing, then returned to her house. I thanked her for the lovely day, and then Lady and I drove back to Los Angeles.

I left for Paris the next day for ten days. I had a great time and returned to a scheduled first real date with Ms. Sake in three days, with the anticipation of a kiss. Ms. New York was leaving me messages while she was on a yacht in the Italian Riviera, wishing I were with her. Ms. Volleyball Player was waiting for my phone call; Ms. Lawyer was expressing an interest in seeing me, and for me to meet her mother, who was visiting in a few days. As if I didn't have enough going on, I browsed the online lesbian ads and found a girl, Ms. Aries, who was hot, sexy, smart and my type, so I e-mailed her before retiring for the evening.

I woke to an e-mail from Ms. Aries. She thought that I was beautiful and wanted to meet me. This shocked me, as she was beautiful, out of most people's league, but she was into me. I showered and was about to head off to work, when Ms. Lawyer started e-mailing me about seeing me this evening. She insisted on coming over to my house to exchange the last of our personal items that were left behind at each other's houses. I'm not sure I trusted her intentions. I suggested that I send a messenger; she declined and agreed to come to my house this evening. *Interesting*, is all I thought.

I went to work, and the e-mails started coming my way from Ms. Sake and Ms. Aries. I tried to back out of my date in three days with Ms.

Sake, due to a recent fever blister. She wouldn't allow it. Then Ms. Aries started in with a bunch of sexy photos. I left work, as Ms. Lawyer was coming to my house within the next hour. I waited for the fateful ending with Ms. Lawyer in person and the final closure of this relationship.

She called. It was the first time in over one month that we had spoken to each other. It was a nice icebreaker. Then she arrived. I wasn't paying attention; my apartment was hot, and I had left the front door open. I was I.M.'ing Ms. Aries when Ms. Lawyer knocked on the door and walked in. I said good-bye to Ms. Aries, and closed the I.M. window while Ms. Lawyer was watching me the entire time. I got up and positioned myself so as not to have to hug her. We both placed our "items" in there proper places on the table. She sat down opposite me. We were both uncomfortable, yet comfortable. She joked that she noticed that I was drinking red wine and not beer. I laughed as if she didn't know me. She said "Where did you put Kristin, as Kristin would never drink red wine?"

I said, "The Kristin that you know is gone and the new Kristin drinks red wine, as did the old Kristin; you just didn't notice." She was puzzled.

We talked about nothing really, just catching up; she received only one phone call throughout this exchange, and was just about to leave when she asked about my future travels. Mind you, earlier I got up to get her some water; she followed me into the kitchen, inspected my computer — was surprised to see that I changed the screensaver from her picture to my dogs. Then she started searching the fridge for new photos. I laughed to myself as there were none.

I finally answered her question about my future travels. I responded, "None work related until October, just personal travel."

She immediately said "What personal travel, who are you visiting and when?"

I was shocked at her boldness; obviously, I didn't want to share by saying personal travel. I said "Portland."

She said "Who is in Portland?" I told her it was my friend. She said "Oh yeah, R------." She became comfortable again. It was none of her business who I was visiting, but I did give her kudos for asking a question that she wanted answered for whatever reason.

We ended our conversation and she got up to leave. I wouldn't go near her to hug her; I just handed her her things, bent down to pet my dog again, and said good-bye impersonally. I wasn't being mean; I just didn't want to hug her good-bye. She looked amazing; she always did to me. Not hugging her good-bye was easier than hugging her good-bye. She got the message, sulked a bit, then left.

I returned to my computer to find Ms. Aries had signed off for the evening. X-#1 was online; we chatted and I sent her some photos of Ms. Aries. She agreed that Aries was hot but not her type, and then she signed off.

I sent Ms. Sake an e-mail, as she was convinced that Ms. Lawyer wanted to reconcile this evening. Maybe that was her intention, maybe that was not her intention; I'm not really sure. Either way, that chapter was closed in my life and I was moving on!

CHAPTER 19

Ms. Aries had been e-mailing lots of photos of herself and I.M.'ing throughout the day. Ms. Sake and I finalized our first "real date" in two days. I hadn't called Ms. Volleyball Player back. I had numerous e-mails. Ms. Beverly Hills had an upcoming birthday and wanted to get together for drinks, as we had talked about the other evening. Ms. New York was leaving messages from Rome, about to come back to the States. X-#1 was inviting me to many social events, and X-#2 was coming back from hiking Mt. Rainier.

I'm tired just thinking about the possibilities, but I liked Ms. Sake, so I didn't make plans with the others or return phone calls or e-mails from potential women.

The day was here for me and Ms. Sake. We were having our first real date. Throughout the past month, we had gone on several "dates" as friends, getting to know one another, but today was our fist real date. She called, we talked, we have decided that I would drive to her house, as she lives about 45 minutes away. We were to go golfing at the driving range, or bowling, and then dinner and a movie at her house—my choice of activities.

Lady and I got in the car, thought about which of the two activities we wanted to partake in; after careful consideration, we chose the golfing range. I parked the car and walked Lady up to her house. She barged in and suddenly I was standing there looking at Ms. Sake. She gave me a sweet hello hug, went back into the kitchen, and asked me which activity I would like to do. I immediately got comfortable, leaned over the counter as she was fluttering about in the kitchen, and said, "Golfing at the golf range." She was relieved that I chose the activity that she wanted to do. *Hmm, note to self, bowling next time to take her out of her comfortable box.*

We grabbed her clubs and headed to the golfing range. We had a charity golf event coming up at work in two weeks and I didn't want to look stupid. More importantly, she wanted to make sure that I wouldn't make a fool out of her, so practice was in order for this kid.

We did just that. Several buckets of balls later, sweat dripping beyond belief (as it was 110 degrees in sunny southern California), we headed back to her house after a lot of fun and a little exercise. She cooked an amazing meal, we drank beer and wine. Her neighbors and their children came in and out throughout the evening; thank goodness for chaperones!

We ate, watched our movie, talked, and hung out. All was well and we were having a splendid time. I was supposed to be the one to make the first move, as I was very shy. She picked up on this a long time ago, so she made me agree to the first move proposal. I agreed to the rules while I was in Paris, but I had a fever blister from our 4th of July weekend and I wouldn't dare try to kiss somebody with a small infection on my lip, so I stayed away. Apparently she didn't mind, because about two in the morning, she had had enough of the friend thing and before I knew it, she got up, straddled me, and started kissing me. I loved it; I was totally into it, and we had a great time making out. Funny, making out—who does that? We fooled around for a few hours and fell asleep on the couch. She woke me up a few hours later with an invitation to her bedroom.

She was really sweet; she gave me a new toothbrush, toothpaste, lounge pants, and a tank top, as I was not planning to spend the night. I got ready for bed, she got ready for bed, we crawled in, fooled around a bit, and then finally crashed about 6 a.m. on Sunday. It was comfortable and wonderful.

Four hours later, we both awoke, started rolling around so as to not wake the other, but clearly wanted to. It was cute and comfortable. I tended to Lady. Ms. Sake tended to her cat. We milled around getting water, brushing teeth, then crawled back into bed and turned the television on. We snuggled up and watched movie after movie after movie all day Sunday. It was the most relaxing and comfortable day I have ever had. We fooled around on and off throughout the day, not too much, but enough. It was awesome.

Finally, about 5 p.m., we decided that we needed to eat. She ordered Thai food to be delivered. We got up and milled around. The neighborhood kids started rolling in, wanting to see Lady. We were famished. She got orange sherbet with chocolate chunks in one bowl with one spoon. She commented on why there was only one spoon. I laughed as she proceeded to feed both her and me the dessert. It was wonderful, something I had never experienced, spoon feeding!

We then went to her back yard. We watched Lady walk around and sat on her swinging chair. She pulled out a book called *Don't Know How She Does It* and started reading several chapters. She looked great, lying on the chair next to me, reading, holding hands, swinging. It was wonderful; I love to read, she loves to read, and having somebody read to you is an incredible, selfless experience!

Lady was apparently the new hot item on the block. The neighborhood kids continued rolling in and out wanting to see her. Our food was delivered. We fed the kids, got the inquisition of why we had a slumber party and they weren't invited. We chuckled; it was cute. We all ate, the kids left, and we crawled back into bed and back to our movie fest.

We were now completely comfortable with each other, snuggled up as a couple, and enjoying the next two shows. She embraced me throughout all of the shows. I snuggled into her body, she kissed my forehead on and off, and touched my arm in an endearing fashion. I started opening up more and more.

Finally it was 12:30 Monday morning. I needed to go home, as we both had a big week ahead of us. I told her that Lady and I needed to leave. She offered for us to stay the evening. I declined, as traffic would be horrendous in the morning versus late in the evening. We started kissing and fooling around, then getting hot and heavy, and we both struggled to not to cross the boundaries of taking things slowly. Finally she said "You need to leave now."

I said, "Two more minutes and we will leave."

Thirty minutes later, she said, "You need to leave now."

I reluctantly agreed, gathered our belongings, gave her a lingering good night kiss at the front door, and Lady and I were driving back to Los Angeles at 1:30 a.m. For the love of love, but it sure was a great weekend.

Lady and I arrived home; she had surgery the next morning. I logged onto the Internet and Ms. New York started I.M.'ing me that she was back in New York after her European vacation. We chatted for awhile before I finally went to bed at 2:30 a.m. I could barely wake up the next morning. I dropped Lady off at the vet and dragged my tired body to work.

Ms. Sake and I e-mailed throughout the day, both expressing our enjoyment of the weekend, priding ourselves on our good behavior, yet both wanting to set a definite future date to see each other next. Meanwhile, both of our work days kicked in. I was in and out of the vet. Finally, early in the evening, we started I.M.'ing each other, talking about our wonderful weekend. We were both smitten with each other!

Apparently my friend and my sister ran into Ms. Lawyer and her mother at a neighborhood watering hole Sunday afternoon. They were in the back room when suddenly they appeared. Greetings were exchanged, future drink plans were made, and both parties were off doing their own thing. Surprisingly, Ms. Lawyer never e-mailed me or mentioned this encounter, as she was busy with her mother; however my friend left me a message stating the facts.

Interesting is what I thought, but I was not fazed, because I was falling for Ms. Sake. I chalked it all up to another day in West Hollywood and went on without an e-mail to Ms. Lawyer mentioning the encounter, as I did not care. Funny how everything works out the way it is supposed to.

CHAPTER 20

Ms. Aries continued to I.M. me and send photos. She was about to take off for the week with her sister to Las Vegas. I've lost interest in her for no other reason than I liked Ms. Sake and I didn't want to waste my energy with others. I don't call Ms. Volleyball Player; Ms. Lawyer and I exchanged a few e-mails back and forth about nothing other than her mother's visit and both of our animals' recent surgeries.

Today I am to meet Ms. Sake and a few others for a business meeting at her casino; we are having an upcoming work event between her casino and my company. I am looking forward to seeing her this afternoon. I woke, showered and tried to look as cute as a girl can when she's about to see her new girl while having to remain professional in a work environment.

I arrived at work and finished some last-minute items before a colleague and I headed to the casino. We arrived early. We walked around with our set designer, doing our own thing, when Ms. Sake walked across the casino floor to meet with us. She sure did look cute, and we kept things professional yet flirty. At one point, we walked by her office. We both were thinking the same thing: how can we lose the others and spend a little alone time together? But that never transpired. We finished our meeting and left.

Back to the office we went. I finished my work and went home. Ms. Sake sent me the following I.M.:

"Ms. Sake: I'm packing up and heading out - taking computer to do pending memo and try and read the 849 messages in my outlook in box! Be back on soon...did I mention how hard it was not to pull you into my office today to be alone?!?"

She then signed off but would return in a few hours. I smiled after reading her I.M. because I had the same thoughts throughout the entire meeting. I liked her; she was awesome and such a great person. I sent her the following e-mail as a response as I waited for her to return online so we could resume our I.M.:

"i am smiling from your im for two reasons...the first your outlook in regard to 849 messages, i can soooo relate, we recently switched from outlook to group-wise, everybody has had tons of problems (i.e. my bosses computer crashed because of it and her hard drive

was replaced today) so instead of dealing with that right before the paris trip, i chose to not even open my group-wise and continued with that plan since i have been back...every time somebody would take a list in regard to their complaints i continued with my staple response 'haven't even opened group-wise, no problems to report at the moment'...well, today my colleague finally snapped with hers and said 'i HATE group-wise, are you having the same problems?'...i looked at her again and said 'honey, i know you think i have been kidding these past 3 weeks but i haven't even opened my group-wise yet, not ready to open that can of worms yet'...she started laughing so hard, almost fell out of her chair and said 'yes, i thought you were exaggerating a bit but actually i can believe it'...i must tackle that beast tomorrow, as my boss's computer is now up and running and i'm sure the e-mails are a flying...

and the second in regard to being alone in your office crossed my mind a few hundred times today...funnier when we returned to the office my boss and colleague both joking implied that and my response was 'b—was a good chaperone, we weren't left alone once'...they both giggled, it was cute, it would have been cuter if k——and b—went off to lunch and left us alone...it's funny both b— and my boss are your biggest fans, not that i am not, as i assure you i am but they keep reminding me of how you are a quality person and for me to not mess this up...jeez, can i have a little credit...if my memory serves me correctly i am the one that FIRST (i need a first for something, work with me here) who told you that i thought you were cute to you and that i had asked a mutual friend to set us up and she wouldn't budge on that topic...i still don't understand that, maybe because at the time i was blowing through women left and right and she didn't want you to be apart of that...so, i guess this shy kid did make the first move looking back and i was the one who told you that i was gay before you ever did...okay, off my soap box...then b—said 'how was your date with ms. sake, i had a dream last night about the 3 of us?'...i said 'really?...it was great, of course it was great'...and she said 'no silly it wasn't that kind of dream, i don't go dreaming of any of your other girls, it was just a dream where we were all sitting around eating, drinking and talking, i really like her and i don't want you to mess this up'...i started laughing...my boss walked in and heard us, she immediately said 'so did you sleep with her?'...i continued to laugh, friends can be so blatant sometimes ...i said 'no, when have i ever just slept with anybody?'...she looked at me and said 'is this an initial liar response or are you being serious?'...i continued to laugh, i had a rough start to my monday being questioned like a fugitive *on the run who was just captured and i said 'no, i'm serious, we are taking things slow, we had a great time'... they both said 'good, you better or you have us to answer to'...we have a girlfriend who is labeled as the initial liar, meaning she goes out with a guy, we know she sleeps with him, immediately denies it, we pull it out of her finally, then i ask the same question 'did you use a condom?'...she immediately says 'yes' and we know she is lying, the truth finally comes out days later, sad yet funny and she is forever labeled as the initial liar...okay more than i'm sure you wanted to know but i had to share, i'm sure your friends questioned you the same as all girlfriends do...i sure do have a bad reputation for only have slept with 4 1/2 women and they know that...i think they get confused because yes i have dated a few women this past year, they have heard those stories and seen the packages that have come through our office, so i can only imagine what their imaginations have conjured up ...but honestly it's in their minds, have i not been nothing but an angel???...well that's pushing it i know but i really am...okay, your eyes are tired, you must go to bed soon but we are on for friday in a public place, since we can't be trusted alone anymore...hmmmm, what does that say...sweet dreams, kc"*

She arrived home shortly, read my e-mail and she sent the following I.M.:

"Ms. Sake: you're not going to ruin this you know...i won't let you.
Kristin: i won't, i promise
Ms. Sake: i know
Ms. Sake: it was interesting to hear you today
Kristin: why?
Ms. Sake: so intelligent and on top of it
Ms. Sake: that was a turn on
Kristin: business settings are cool that way
Ms. Sake: yeah
Kristin: i couldn't agree more
Kristin: funny how that happens
Kristin: another layer as you would say
Ms. Sake: i thought it would be more disconnected
Ms. Sake: but that morning i was actually excited that you were coming
Kristin: it was my job to make sure that it wasn't
Kristin: me too
Ms. Sake: it was all good"

Work conversation took place; then the following transpired:

"Kristin: how can i help?
Kristin: take your mind off work
Kristin: i can do that
Ms. Sake: you are doing it
Kristin: good, smiling i hope
Ms. Sake: yes
Kristin: good
Kristin: me too
Ms. Sake: good, i love it when you smile
Ms. Sake: very pretty...
Kristin: funny, i do it a lot actually
Kristin: good
Ms. Sake: so do i —i love to laugh
Ms. Sake: but we already know that
Kristin: yes you do and good at it
Kristin: yes we do
Kristin: balance
Ms. Sake: yep
Kristin: it's all about balance
Kristin: a lesson i am learning
Ms. Sake: that's another lesson
Kristin: mind reader
Ms. Sake: i know
Ms. Sake: that happens a lot with us"

We had a discussion about what one wanted versus expected from a person. Long story short, I cut to the chase and asked the following question:

"Kristin: so, what do you expect out of me?
Kristin: let's start here
Ms. Sake: nothing
Kristin: let's talk about us
Kristin: nothing, honey i have a story for you
Ms. Sake: life lesson number 1210
Kristin: expect nothing and you get nothing
Ms. Sake: don't expect anything, and you won't be disappointed
Kristin: have a little hope or desire and you might get something
Ms. Sake: no
Kristin: don't expect and you are correct you won't get disappointed
Kristin: can i share a story with you, one i learned
Kristin: the hard way
Ms. Sake: k
Kristin: first love and i broke up

Kristin: i was with x #1
Kristin: x#1 and i broke up
Kristin: i wanted to go away for a weekend alone to regroup
Kristin: first love and i were friends
Kristin: she was going thru a breakup and long story short ended up spending the weekend with me
Kristin: i picked her up and we were off for a weekend alone to recover
Kristin: immediately she fell into the comfort zone of us
Kristin: loved it
Kristin: flirting the entire car ride, everything, no stops
Kristin: i loved it
Kristin: we get to the hotel
Kristin: check in
Kristin: we get to the room
Kristin: she starts kissing me, hugging me, making all of the moves
Kristin: she stopped me and said 'what do you expect to happen this weekend?'
Kristin: i took the safe route and said 'i expect nothing'
Kristin: she looked at me and said 'you expect nothing, if you get more then that is a bonus?'
Kristin: i said 'yes'
Kristin: she would have nothing to do with me
Kristin: the rest of the weekend
Kristin: she punished me
Kristin: then
Kristin: we were 15 minutes out of new orleans
Kristin: when my phone started ringing from x#1
Kristin: first love got jealous
Kristin: and said 'will you go on a real date with me this evening?'
Kristin: and i said 'yes'
Kristin: the bullshit was dropped
Kristin: and finally i expected something and got something, i put myself out there
Kristin: that was the last evening we spent together
Kristin: so lesson was learned the hard way here
Ms. Sake: wait one minute
Ms. Sake: you told the truth
Ms. Sake: you expected nothing - you WANTED something
Ms. Sake: there's a huge difference
Kristin: it was implied
Ms. Sake: she held
Ms. Sake: wait
Ms. Sake: you hostage for that
Ms. Sake: made you pay

Kristin: it was the same thing, she wanted me to say that and i wouldn't let myself be vulnerable

Ms. Sake: then got jealous because of x#1 and felt she might take you away and then dropped the bullshit

Kristin: that's all i am saying, it's not fair to hold back when you really want something

Kristin: she wanted me to say that i loved her from the beginning

Ms. Sake: i didn't say i didn't want anything!

Ms. Sake: but I don't expect anything

Ms. Sake: i won't pigeon hole you that way

Kristin: i guess i am incorrect because wanting and expecting are the same to me

Ms. Sake: i can't predict or control you

Kristin: why not want and expect the same thing?

Ms. Sake: that would be expecting you to act in a certain way or do a certain thing - very similar to assuming

Kristin: it's about being vulnerable and being honest

Ms. Sake: because we are not the same

Ms. Sake: asking for what you want is the hardest thing to do and makes you very vulnerable... to rejection

Ms. Sake: that's why we don't do it

Ms. Sake: but we always expect people to do certain things and then hold them accountable when they don't deliver

Ms. Sake: you can't know me yet

Kristin: to me it's the same

Ms. Sake: you think you do

Ms. Sake: you want to

Kristin: i guess i am incorrect

Ms. Sake: no, we just disagree

Kristin: i see that

Ms. Sake: so, what do you expect from me?

Ms. Sake: and i'll tell you what i want from you

Kristin: you just said the two were different, so what do you want to know expect or want from you?

Ms. Sake: to you they are same

Kristin: correct but i'm asking you because they are different to you?

Ms. Sake: right, but when you tell me what you expect, i know it is also what you want because you have told me the two are the same.

Ms. Sake: you already know i expect nothing from you, but i will tell you what i want, because to me there is a difference

Kristin: you are correct, you will get the same answer

Kristin: what i want and expect from you is the following

Kristin: honesty

Kristin: intimacy but not false intimacy and time will allow for that to happen

64

Kristin: laughter
Ms. Sake: agreement over here
Kristin: good, i like that
Kristin: respect
Kristin: trust
Ms. Sake: can i interject for a moment
Kristin: yes
Ms. Sake: don't worry about the intimacy
Ms. Sake: we've had fantastic intimacy so far
Kristin: i concur
Ms. Sake: what's better than spending the whole day together holding each other and touching and laughing and sharing?
Kristin: i couldn't agree more
Ms. Sake: all of my friends know that i am very slow
Kristin: but you already knew that
Ms. Sake: the joke is i move so slow i almost move backwards
Kristin: nothing wrong with that, then you picked the right subject
Ms. Sake: that's because the last couple of times i was with someone I didn't sleep with them right away
Ms. Sake: in fact, i didn't sleep with some of them and it took a lot of time for others.
Kristin: i understand, nothing wrong with that
Ms. Sake: even with the ones I stayed with for years, it took a while
Ms. Sake: i don't give my body to just anyone either
Ms. Sake: that's not what it's for
Kristin: we are on the same page
Kristin: part of the attraction
Kristin: so you have nothing to explain
Kristin: i know that
Kristin: i like that
Kristin: i feel no pressure
Ms. Sake: i know
Kristin: again, a lot of why i am comfortable with you
Kristin: as i don't pressure you
Ms. Sake: yeah...i get that
Ms. Sake: also
Kristin: good
Ms. Sake: if we were to repeat patterns
Ms. Sake: or repeat patterns we see
Ms. Sake: i would have been at your house already
Ms. Sake: i wouldn't put so much time between us
Ms. Sake: because too many, time is scary
Kristin: i agree
Ms. Sake: distance is scary

Kristin: i disagree

Kristin: it is or it isn't

Ms. Sake: it translates to the fact that you don't want to be here so you must not want me

Kristin: that's what time and distance tells one

Kristin: people think that but that is not true

Ms. Sake: lots of time and distance - agreed

Kristin: the mind alone is a wonderful tool

Ms. Sake: i think its a compliment for us

Ms. Sake: we have full lives

Kristin: i agree

Kristin: we do

Ms. Sake: and we want to do other things with other people

Kristin: yes we do

Ms. Sake: and then meet later and reconnect and be intimate and share

Kristin: nothing wrong with that

Ms. Sake: personally, i can't wait to see you Friday

Kristin: eventually those lives mesh or they don't

Kristin: that's the bottom line

Ms. Sake: it is making my week go much quicker

Kristin: i can't wait either and that is awesome

Ms. Sake: and i can't stop thinking about it

Ms. Sake: and i don't even know what we are going to do

Kristin: me too and the week does go quicker

Ms. Sake: well, sort of

Kristin: i'll tell you what we are doing tomorrow

Kristin: my turn

Ms. Sake: yes

Kristin: i have it planned out already

Kristin: shocker i know

Kristin: don't start with me

Kristin: you are kind of like the school yard bully

Kristin: scared, commitaphobic is want you want me to say

Kristin: but i won't

Kristin: i won't give you that because you are not

Kristin: you are just scared like the rest of us

Kristin: that's normal, did i use that word, i think i did

Kristin: and that is okay

Kristin: sit with those feelings and you will like how you are feeling or you will leave

Kristin: no worries here

Kristin: that doesn't scare me

Kristin: it is or it isn't

Kristin: no pressures from me

Kristin: you won't get that because that is not my nature
Kristin: one wants to be in or out
Kristin: no in between
Ms. Sake: i don't feel like you are commitaphobic at all
Kristin: i'm not
Ms. Sake: in fact, i get the sense you commit very much
Kristin: i do
Kristin: and i want that
Kristin: that's just me
Ms. Sake: and you have a good sense of what is worth committing to
Kristin: i do
Kristin: i've been in touch with that early on
Kristin: it's a good thing, that's why i am different
Kristin: i want somebody who wants to be with me
Ms. Sake: i also don't get the sense that you are scared
Kristin: for who i am, no pretenses
Ms. Sake: at all
Kristin: i'm not scared of that at all
Kristin: i want that and i will get that
Ms. Sake: you want me to tell you exactly
Kristin: yeap
Kristin: no bullshit
Kristin: honesty
Ms. Sake: no bullshit
Kristin: the truth isn't always easy
Kristin: but better than bullshit
Kristin: it's not bad, it just is
Ms. Sake: k
Kristin: i agree
Ms. Sake: my sense of you, based on what i know of you is simple
Ms. Sake: you are a learner
Ms. Sake: you are a sponge
Kristin: i am
Ms. Sake: you grow
Ms. Sake: hey stop and listen
Ms. Sake: you grow from watching
Ms. Sake: watching has made you very smart about behaviors and patterns
Ms. Sake: in others
Ms. Sake: your own personal growth has come from your experiences
Ms. Sake: but not necessarily from personal relationships
Ms. Sake: more family oriented
Ms. Sake: you are your youngest at personal relationships
Ms. Sake: you forgive a lot more behaviors in lovers than family
Ms. Sake: you expect more

Ms. Sake: from family
Ms. Sake: you are an introvert
Ms. Sake: homebody
Ms. Sake: you would rather be alone
Ms. Sake: but someone or something moved you to try something different
Ms. Sake: i can't tell if it was someone or an event - maybe your coming out
Ms. Sake: now you want to taste life
Ms. Sake: you grabbed onto social outings and events like they were very important
Ms. Sake: you got huge lessons out of the smallest of experiences with others
Ms. Sake: hold on i have to plug in
Kristin: battery dying, such is the life of a lesbian
Kristin: you are correct in everything you have said
Ms. Sake: what was a normal social outing for most
Ms. Sake: left a huge impression on you
Ms. Sake: because you want
Ms. Sake: you want to have that experience
Ms. Sake: actually
Ms. Sake: you want to have options
Ms. Sake: to partake or walk away
Ms. Sake: sometimes its fun
Ms. Sake: but you get more out of intimate settings
Ms. Sake: you do one or two far better that a room full
Ms. Sake: you don't do small talk
Ms. Sake: it's a waste and seems so artificial
Ms. Sake: but it's a nice suit to try on and walk around in every once in a while
Ms. Sake: just to prove you can
Kristin: you have my number that is for sure
Kristin: with that information what do you want from me?
Ms. Sake: i want you to be yourself
Ms. Sake: i don't want to be surprised later
Ms. Sake: i can be pleasantly surprised
Ms. Sake: that you have interesting layers that aren't unhealthy or mean spirited
Ms. Sake: i want you to be comfortable
Ms. Sake: i want you to enjoy your own space
Ms. Sake: i want you to get me
Ms. Sake: i want you to push me away if i crowd you
Ms. Sake: i want us to support each other in our decisions and life choices
Ms. Sake: i want us to take it all in
Ms. Sake:: i want us to breathe in synch
Ms. Sake: i want you to tell me when you are afraid

Ms. Sake: angry

Ms. Sake: lonely

Ms. Sake: sad

Ms. Sake: happy

Ms. Sake: joyful

Ms. Sake: uncertain or unclear

Ms. Sake: i want you to be blown away

Ms. Sake: i want to know your core

Ms. Sake: i want us to come home

Ms. Sake: i want to be a safe place for you

Ms. Sake: but i don't expect you to want the same

Kristin: funny you should write that last line, i will delete that as i want nothing more than what you just described

Kristin: and i can do that

Kristin: believe it or not

Ms. Sake: but kristin

Kristin: but what?

Ms. Sake: we are human

Kristin: what you just described is not obtainable?

Ms. Sake: and there is one fault i know i have that i can easily express

Kristin: in anyway

Ms. Sake: sometimes i'm sloppy

Kristin: which is what?

Ms. Sake: i always mean well, but i don't always do it with perfection

Kristin: thank goodness

Ms. Sake: i'll leak all over you

Kristin: i don't want a perfectionist i tell you

Kristin: NEVER

Ms. Sake: and move through it like jell-o

Ms. Sake: and say the wrong thing

Kristin: perfectionist is an evil word...lol

Kristin: sister is a perfectionist and i see the daily pain she lives with

Ms. Sake: i learned that lesson early on

Kristin: me too, not me nor do i want that in my partner

Kristin: stressful

Ms. Sake: we must let go of the life we have planned so as to live the life we were meant to

Ms. Sake: that is why i don't believe in expectations

Kristin: exactly

Ms. Sake: they are plans

Ms. Sake: i must accept you for who you are

Kristin: i disagree but that is okay

Kristin: yes you must

Ms. Sake: true

Kristin: i am no angel
Kristin: but i try
Ms. Sake: thank god
Ms. Sake: so
Kristin: so
Ms. Sake: can we go on a REAL DATE now!!!
Ms. Sake: lol
Kristin: what is the definition of that?
Kristin: i like your definitions...
Kristin: i'm the one in charge of friday evening
Kristin: so you must let the planner know what the expectations are
Kristin: no pun intended
Ms. Sake: okay
Ms. Sake: can i tell you what i had planned?
Kristin: no because i have it planned but you can tell me what you want
Kristin: see i listen
Ms. Sake: i want casual
Ms. Sake: i want to hold your hand
Ms. Sake: i want to talk
Ms. Sake: i want to share my thoughts and yours
Ms. Sake: i want to kiss
Ms. Sake: a lot
Ms. Sake: i want to hold you
Ms. Sake: and listen to you breathe
Ms. Sake: i want to laugh
Ms. Sake: i want to feel that flutter
Ms. Sake: i want to pay my bills - just checking to see if you are paying
        attention
Kristin: you will have all of the above, except you are on your own for the
        last item
Ms. Sake: darn
Kristin: i have to do the same tomorrow, life
Kristin: but
Kristin: butterflies in the stomach are a nice feeling
Kristin: that's the beauty of one's mind
Kristin: to recreate
Kristin: those feelings
Ms. Sake: absolutely
Ms. Sake: to create those feelings
Kristin: exactly, just seeing if you are paying attention
Ms. Sake: always
Kristin: that's a good sign
Kristin: as i you
Ms. Sake: so...you know what time it is again?

Kristin: i do and i can't be held accountable that's on you as i stated earlier
Kristin: but yes it is late
Kristin: i'll let you retire
Ms. Sake: i don't want you to let me go
Kristin: i won't
Ms. Sake: i want you to say goodnight until tomorrow
Kristin: just for the evening as i don't want to ruin your day tomorrow
Kristin: sweet dreams until tomorrow
Kristin: we are on the same page
Ms. Sake: sweet dreams to you
Kristin: no worries
Ms. Sake: ain't that great?!?
Kristin: it certainly is
Kristin: sweet dreams
Kristin: goodbye, sign off
Kristin: lol
Ms. Sake: k
Kristin: goodnight until tomorrow"

CHAPTER 21

I last left off with the lovely I.M. with Ms. Sake, and in two days we are to have another "real date" with no sex, as that is always a bad thing to rush into when you really like somebody. She is driving up to my house; we are going to dinner, a movie, and then back to my house for the evening.

I go to work and I.M. Ms. Sake throughout the day with great anticipation of our upcoming date. We get through the work day being everything but productive. I go home, log on to my computer, and receive an I.M. from X-#2. We talked about both of our new girlfriends, as we are friends now, very happy for that. She invited me to see her last soccer game on Saturday if my date doesn't run into that day, as I'm sure it will but it was a nice gesture either way. Ms. New York and I I.M. a little bit, and I am just about to log off shortly before midnight, when Ms. Lawyer suddenly I.M.'s me and the following transpires:

"Ms. Lawyer: it's official......the kitty is a lap kitty. what a mama's boy!!!!
Kristin: wow, really?
Kristin: send him home with your mother
Kristin: before he changes
Ms. Lawyer: it's insane.
Kristin: he is such a baby
Ms. Lawyer: i would rather send syd home with her.
Kristin: wait
Kristin: don't sell syd out that soon
Kristin: he is ill, wounded and wanting, needing (kneeding) no pun intended
Ms. Lawyer: not really......he is all healed.
Ms. Lawyer: jumping around from one lap to the other.
Kristin: i don't believe it
Ms. Lawyer: syd is hissing like it's her job.
Kristin: one month from today i want to hear the same thing
Ms. Lawyer: no one believes it till they see it.
Kristin: nope
Ms. Lawyer: k... i will put it in my calendar.
Kristin: one month from today, thank you
Kristin: pen this in, not pencil

We switched topics from the kitten being neutered to the war in Iraq; then the following transpired:

Kristin: u never knew my position
Kristin: or party
Kristin: silence is golden
Ms. Lawyer: democrat and proud of it
Kristin: i know u are
Ms. Lawyer: sometimes
Ms. Lawyer: re: silence
Kristin: i will answer that question in the future
Kristin::)
Kristin: ask
Kristin: not answer
Ms. Lawyer: yeah...i ask why any gay woman can be a republican
Kristin: good question feisty one
Kristin: statement actually
Kristin: i'm not fighting this fight with you
Kristin: pick another topic not this one
Ms. Lawyer: i know you are a republican......we could never have lasted......
Kristin: you are correct in that we could never have lasted but not for that
          reason
Kristin: many others
Kristin: not that one
Ms. Lawyer: well hopefully we can be friends.
Kristin: we are friends, i have NO hard feelings one bit
Kristin: as you should not
Kristin: we were just different
Ms. Lawyer: none on my part at all
Kristin: we were bed buddies
Kristin: nothing more from your point of view
Kristin: mine was different but you got caught up in something different
Ms. Lawyer: not really even that
Kristin: k
Kristin: emotional crutch
Kristin: i got that from the get go
Kristin: ask m————our first night at the belmont
Kristin: i called it
Kristin: not to bring poker in the arena
Kristin: god forbid i have wit
Ms. Lawyer: i didn't mean it that way...but according to you, we didn't have
          enough sex to be bed buddies
Ms. Lawyer: let's not get into this... i think you are great. we just weren't
          great together. it has very little to do with where i am emotionally
Kristin: you are correct and i don't want to get into this
Ms. Lawyer: i appreciate all that you were to me and for me...you opened
          my eyes, kristin.

Kristin: it is only important because we never really talked about it
Kristin: that's all
Kristin: i have moved on
Kristin: i actually have a girlfriend
Kristin: but i was curious what your take on this was
Ms. Lawyer: as do i
Kristin: that's all
Kristin: so it's all good
Ms. Lawyer: but, i am willing to talk to you about us if you want, but just not right now, because my mom is here and so is she.
Kristin: no hard feelings, just curious
Kristin: cool
Ms. Lawyer: actually, i think we should talk about it at some point...just at a later date.
Kristin: good night
Ms. Lawyer: talk soon."

So we ended our I.M. I sent her an e-mail asking her to tell me when things were over for her, as we have never discussed that, and for some reason I needed to know that, in order for me to move on completely. I signed off and went to bed for the evening. Internet dating can be very tiring sometimes but hopefully worth it in the long run; only time will tell.

CHAPTER 22

It was now Friday and I was excited for my long-awaited date this evening with Ms. Sake. We were both giddy with excitement. We e-mailed and I.M.'ed throughout the afternoon like little kids, when suddenly I received an I.M. from Ms. Aries, inviting me to San Diego Pride with her and her sister this weekend. I politely declined, as I had other plans. She asked if we could meet in person one day. I didn't know what to say; I didn't want to be rude, but I didn't want to give her false hope. I am off the market permanently because of Ms. Sake, but she doesn't know that yet! I responded with, "Yes, that would be nice. Whenever you are in Los Angeles, let me know, and if I'm in San Diego, I will let you know." I ended it by saying I needed to get back to my work. She got the message and it was over before it ever started.

It was at that point that I officially knew that my love at online lesbian dating was over. I was falling for Ms. Sake and I knew that my online dating must be terminated. I logged onto love at online lesbian dating, pulled up my account, went through the existing procedures, assuring them that I had met my future partner through their services, and terminated my membership. I didn't tell anybody, as I didn't want to, but I knew in my heart that it was time to end this relationship. I had met Ms. Sake, somebody who had blown me away in all aspects.

I completed my work, headed home, and waited as Ms. Sake was on her way to my house. There was a knock at the door. I answered it. She was standing in the doorway looking amazing. I drank her in for a moment. She walked in, put her hand on the lower curve of my back, drew me into her, and we had a passionate long overdue kiss.

After coming up for air I handed her the parking pass to hang from her rearview mirror so she wouldn't get another parking ticket. She scurried off to do that. I finished getting ready, and she returned. We laughed, drank wine, made out on the couch, missed our dinner reservations and almost missed our movie, when we decided to peel ourselves off of each other and leave for the movie.

We walked across the street, purchased our tickets and a popcorn and Milk Duds dinner. We snuggled into a French movie with English subtitles. The 90-minute movie flew by; it was not good, but it was perfect. We ate popcorn and Milk Duds, held hands, laughed, and had an incredible time. The movie ended, and we walked home, sat and looked at each other as if to ask *what next?* I asked her if she wanted to get sushi or rent a movie, or we could do whatever she wanted to do. She looked at me and said, "I am fine right where I am."

I said, "Good, me too," and we snuggled back into the couch, talking, laughing, listening to music, and making out until about 4 a.m. Finally we retired to my bedroom. She undressed into her pajamas as did I; we made out a little bit, then fell asleep listening to Norah Jones with candles in the background. It was wonderful and we sleep well together.

I woke at 9 a.m. because I needed to walk my dog—not because I was uncomfortable, since I wasn't. I walked Lady, then brought the fan into the bedroom because it was ungodly hot. I brushed my teeth, got us both water, and then snuggled up next to her. She was nothing but accepting of my touch and it was amazing. We lay in bed all afternoon, laughing, talking, hugging, making out; it was incredible. Somebody knocked on the door around 11 a.m. and she said, "Oh good, my surprise is here." Apparently, the previous day, she had placed an order from the local grocery store to deliver our breakfast for the day and food for the week. (I do not shop.) She cooked an incredible breakfast. We ate and then retired back to the bedroom for the rest of the afternoon.

It was a wonderful day. We basically had sex fully clothed. I looked at her at one point and said, "Is this how you take things slowly?"

She laughed and said, "No, Kristin, this is not taking things slowly. I don't know what you do to me, but I assure you I am on my best behavior. I know that I want you and you me, so it's all good."

I laughed and said, "Clearly. Just checking, because this is not what I would consider taking things slowly."

She said, "Do you want me to slow down?"

I said, "No, this is perfect!" We laughed because our big joke is how I am shy and how she takes things so slowly that she actually moves backwards. Well, not the case here!

We both felt the connection. In fact, it's the first time since my first love that I had literally "had the shakes." I shared that I had not felt that in a very long time. She asked, "Since when?"

I said, "I'm not telling you, other than a long time." She smiled and understood. More importantly, I felt something that I have never felt before, and that was scary, yet enticing. We had a fabulous day and before we knew it, it was 6 p.m. My sister was calling me to meet her for drinks, and Ms. Sake had to go meet her friend. We didn't want to let each other go, but we had to pry ourselves apart, as painful as it was.

She packed up to leave. We said good-bye. We were barely able to pull ourselves apart from each other, but we had to. We agreed to meet the following day for a concert in Hermosa Beach. Lady and I walked her to her car. She proceeded to give me two CDs to listen to in order for me to "get her." I accepted them and said good-bye, thinking how cute she looked and thinking that I just wanted to grab her and kiss her. But I didn't, I backed off. I wished her well, she pulled away, and we waved good-bye. Lady and I walked back up to the apartment.

I missed her already. I called my sister and my friend, explained that I was running late, and eventually passed on the get-together, as I was tired, missed Ms. Sake, and wanted nothing more than to crawl into bed.

I drove to the store, returned, and logged on to find an e-mail from Ms. Lawyer. I had forgotten that I had asked her for her closure in a previous e-mail days ago. It was a nice e-mail, telling me where she thought things went wrong, how we both are seeing other people and that she hoped that we could remain friends. I thanked her for her response, expressed how we were friends, no hard feelings, and that we have moved through our transition period and are good to go.

I put in Ms. Sake's CDs; I was curious as to what kind of music moved her. It was meaningful, rhythmatic music. I sat down to write another chapter. Then I heard this amazing song that Ms. Sake asked me to listen to. It was a song from Linda Eder's *Gold* CD, song number 7. It said that one needs to allow the love in again and to believe in love again. The lyrics tapped into my soul and played on the strings of my heart. This song moved me; in fact, this entire album moved me.

I loved her for sharing that song which represented the core of my being. While listening to this song for the third time, I received a text message from Ms. Sake saying "Miss you." I responded with "I miss you more, thank you for the fabulous day, can't wait for tomorrow, wish you were in my bed right now."

Isn't love grand? So I sat listening to her CD, thinking about our future, and knowing that finally, I had come home!

CHAPTER 23

Ms. Sake and I exchanged flirtatious e-mails throughout the following day. We both wanted nothing more than to be in each other's presence, but knew that we had a long work week ahead of us. We agreed to get together one "school night" this week, that I would spend the evening, so we waited with great anticipation.

E-mails were exchanged throughout the afternoon. Eventually, I invited her to take an upcoming trip to Aruba. She agreed but fought me on the payment issue. We had our first fight. How cute! But she will come, as I wanted her to. She informed me that she will and that she knew a long time ago, before I even knew that I was going to invite her. I didn't doubt it for one second, as we were on the same page completely. I wanted her there more than I even knew; all I knew is that I wanted her there with me.

We finished the day e-mailing about upcoming events. X-#2 I.M.'ed me, inviting me to coffee and I agreed. We are friends now, and I sensed something was up, not sure what, but knew it was time to finally meet for coffee. I got pulled away with work; the evening dragged on, and I got home late. X-#2 called, and we agreed for her to pick me up. She came to my house. We said hello and hugged, and then I asked her if she was hungry; I was starving. She said yes, and we headed off to dinner. We had a good time reminiscing. I got grilled a lot, sucked it up, pretended that I didn't get what it was she was saying. We both talked about ex-girlfriends since us, our new loves and our past experiences. It was actually nice and comfortable as we were now friends.

We ate and then left. She wanted to extend it to coffee, but I said, "No, I have somebody that I need to get back to." She understood, and gave me a CD that she made for me called "Was it Love?" I accepted it gracefully, knowing that the answer to that question was no. I gave her a hug, noticing the shooting pain in my back from my previous weekend's touching and hugging fest. I smiled and said good night.

I entered my apartment and found Lady happy to see me. I put in the CD and logged on to find the following e-mail from Ms. Sake:

*"...btw, real quick - I just wanted to let you know that you are **not** paying for Aruba, at least not for me. I won't stand for that, I would think you know that about me already!! That's not fair to you and, while probably one of the most awesome gestures I have ever*

received, I appreciate it but I cannot accept it. You are someone I really want to spend more time with, like a lot of time with, so this trip is for both of us. Listen, I canceled my New Zealand trip so this is going to take the place of it (of course you know that now you have to pretend to be a couple and fight intermittently - you can handle that can't you?)

Babe, we have a very long time ahead of us to get to know and shower gifts upon each other... this is far too much but I sure do want to show you how I feel inside about the offer!!

On another note, the weather is freaky right now. We just had the biggest lightning bolt and clap of thunder hit right outside our casino - scared me!! The computer keeps going down because of it - or it's the co-generation plant exploding, don't tell B--- I don't want her to panic.

Okay you. I should be done here in about an hour and on my way home...thinking about your face and how badly I want to be touching it right about now...xxox ms. sake"

My immediate response to her was via e-mail, before I enticed her with a text message saying that I sent her an e-mail to see how impetuous she was to read it. It took her about two minutes to log on after receiving the text message to read the following e-mail from me:

*"btw, you are uninvited to aruba if what i read is correct but i'll let you rethink the **ORIGINAL** offer and **NOT** your counter offer...this was my idea, something that i want to do for both of us (i like you get self gratification from certain things and this is one of those things) and you have to trust that i will follow through with all of the details, that equates to you having to give up complete control and trust me...hm, can ms. sake do that???...now that is the ten million dollar question...i'm a betting girl and i trust that you will be able to get out of your box (didn't you learn anything from tony robbins?), give kristin your travel dates and obtain a passport in a timely manner, just my bet, you are worth the gamble, so ante up the items that i have requested...enough said about this topic and i don't anticipate us fighting intermittently, i understand not the normal display of 'lesbian affection' but if you must play this game consider this our first fight!!!...when do we get to make up???...that's the best part of this, making up and going to aruba together, the choice is yours, not mine as i took the chance and made the offer...and if you play your cards right, the cancellation of*

79

your new zealand trip may just be a postponement until next september and in addition a paris trip next july...just a hunch, so start saving your pennies darling as i love to travel and take my luver with me...hmmm, you may just have a passport already if you were going to new zealand shortly, so all you need to do is give up your dates but me knowing you like i know you, you never obtained that passport, now you have something to do:):):)

and yes we have a very long time ahead of us and traveling together will be nothing but sheer joy for both of us, that much i already know and i can't wait to show you the island of aruba...for one there is this great little church in the middle of nowhere that i can't wait to show you, it was similar to the one in the french movie that we saw but with the most amazing breath of salt in the air that you breathe in, the ocean waves crashing around you as it is located on the rough side of the island, not a soul around, this little stone church sitting alone in the middle of nowhere—it's awesome is all that i can say...i guess having lesbian sex in this church is sacrilegious but then again what religion are you???...okay mind is coming out of the gutter, no pun intended, well sort of, okay out of the gutter...then there is this fabulous lighthouse, sitting alone on this point that overlooks, yes you guessed it the ocean, fantastic is all that i can say...something that i don't need to mention, the prettiest blue water on this planet, with the whitest purest sand, you will think that you are in heaven, i promise you that much...and there is a gay restaurant/bar just outside our hotel, we might even be able to dance with one another in a public place, go figure, not that we need that but the option is there if we want to do that...maybe we should wait and have sex in aruba for our first time???...okay, i got caught up in the entire aruba fantasy for the moment but that is ridiculous, as if either one of us can wait until october for that but we can continue on there but only if you agree to come...please tell me that you are smiling from ear to ear by now, of course you are, how could you not ante up to this trip of a lifetime???...why are you still reading this i should have had you at 'btw'...now that's my girl...you had no clue what you were getting into with me, did you???...a pleasant surprise i hope, yes a pleasant surprise for both of us, what took us so long???...ahhhh, yes that fateful thing called timing...i get that more now than ever, everything is lined up perfectly for both of us, amazing is all that i can say...

now back to the freaky weather, another tell sign if the witch in me must say...scary in one sense but terribly romantic in another sense, if i must state the obvious but with you i do not...did i ever share with you that lying in bed with your luv-er during a rain storm, windows and screen doors opened, listening to the wind whistling, the rain drops falling down around you is one of the most sensual experiences on this earth?...at least in my mind it is...there is nothing better says my lip making that sound as i type this...and meaning every part of it...ahhhh, do i wish more than ever to be in your bed curled up with you at this very moment...the cool breeze for the first time this past month, our bodies naked next to each other, kissing each others lips and bodies pressing against each other...not sure i can think of anything better, can you???

okay you, i think i have tortured us both enough for another evening, how soon until we both implode? (another favorite word of mine)...how badly i want to be touching your face, breasts, outer leg, etc...right about now...lip making that noise, hm, you sure have gotten the best of me and i you, nothing better than knowing that, trusting that and sharing that...sweet dreams, kc"

She read my e-mail and then we started I.M.'ing —the first part got cut off but we eventually got to the following I.M.:

"Kristin: i don't operate that way
Kristin: exactly
Kristin: we both know that
Kristin: and we aren't afraid to talk about it, share it or feel it
Ms. Sake: and there is so much time to discover that for ourselves, because we earned this
Kristin: that's how it should be
Kristin: you are correct, alone and together
Ms. Sake: true
Ms. Sake: we are right for each other
Kristin: we are
Ms. Sake: on many levels
Kristin: and we both know it on all levels
Ms. Sake: in many ways
Kristin: most don't get one level
Ms. Sake: true
Kristin: we see that
Kristin: b/c of what we have experienced
Kristin: that is the beauty of timing
Kristin: and experience
Ms. Sake: i keep thinking about how we kiss...
Kristin: it's amazing, huh?

81

Ms. Sake: i've said it before - I'm a kisser
Kristin: me too
Ms. Sake: by nature that is my favorite thing to do
Kristin: i agree
Kristin: and breathing
Ms. Sake: i can't believe it when others don't get that
Kristin: touching
Ms. Sake: so I have had other experiences
Ms. Sake: but none compare to you
Kristin: and you have learned
Ms. Sake: do you know why?
Kristin: what you want and don't want
Kristin: why?
Ms. Sake: you need to guess at least one time
Kristin: because i get you and we are two peas in a pod with the same feelings
Kristin: in the intimacy
Kristin: it's about intimacy not sex
Kristin: that's a bonus
Kristin: the connection
Kristin: did i guess it?
Ms. Sake: Because with you i don't need it...i want it
Kristin: desire it
Kristin: crave it
Ms. Sake: yes
Kristin: yes i understand
Kristin: clearly
Kristin: have i felt this way before?
Kristin: secret
Ms. Sake: i don't need it to make you understand or desire me
Kristin: nope
Ms. Sake: i want it because it makes me feel good
Kristin: exactly
Ms. Sake: and when we are there
Kristin: it's a great feeling
Ms. Sake: there is nothing better
Kristin: you can never get enough, me neither, that's a great thing
Ms. Sake: its an accepting
Ms. Sake: because of your whole breathing experience
Kristin: 100%
Ms. Sake: i fall in
Kristin: as you should
Ms. Sake: and you take me somewhere
Kristin: i'm happy for that

Ms. Sake: somewhere where it is easy to give in
Kristin: as you do me
Kristin: good
Kristin: people think it's supposed to be work
Ms. Sake: i'm not quite as subtle as you
Kristin: when it shouldn't be
Kristin: i'm not subtle
Kristin: you know me
Ms. Sake: yes, you are
Kristin: you know i'm in 500%
Kristin: do you not know that i am there?
Kristin: with all or nothing?
Ms. Sake: it's not about percentages
Kristin: answer that
Kristin: am i totally connected with you in all aspects?
Ms. Sake: the reason i can go there is because you have those subtle, but distinct clues
Kristin: then it's not subtle but i understand what you are saying
Kristin: i let you know but in all the right ways
Kristin: not too much and not too little
Ms. Sake: correct
Kristin: it's an art in getting to know you
Ms. Sake: that's now our language
Kristin: exactly
Kristin: it's wonderful
Ms. Sake: we are developing our communication
Kristin: i can take you to a new place as well as you taking me to a new place
Kristin: what more could one desire
Ms. Sake: i can be driving and in my inner mind i can hear your breathing and i shiver
Kristin: good, as i you
Ms. Sake: so what's the point? you ask
Kristin: it's such a powerful feeling
Kristin: i don't ask but share
Ms. Sake: we are equals
Ms. Sake: partners
Kristin: absolutely
Kristin: yes
Kristin: as it should be
Ms. Sake: in every sense of the word
Kristin: yes
Ms. Sake: so why should you take on this trip
Kristin: something neither one has experienced

Ms. Sake: alone
Ms. Sake: when you actually have to work
Kristin: because i can spend time with you and work
Ms. Sake: a true partnership
Kristin: what a better experience
Kristin: in a true partnership
Kristin: if you must ask
Ms. Sake: would see the one who doesn't have a show to manage
Kristin: i get the best of both worlds
Ms. Sake: take on the bulk of responsibility
Ms. Sake: because they can
Kristin: you have to wait on the beautiful beaches while i work
Kristin: poor you
Ms. Sake: and next time it will be up to you
Kristin: honestly, listen
Kristin: stop and listen
Kristin: if u must make me talk rationally and i didn't want to have to do this
Kristin: but i will
Kristin: listen
Kristin: you will have to take one week vacation
Kristin: which costs you time and money
Kristin: stop
Kristin: listen
Kristin: in return, i am at a work function of which they pay for me to get there
Kristin: i will get a great deal on a hotel
Kristin: and your airfare i can either pay for or use mileage
Kristin: so it's NOT about money
Kristin: but since you made me go there i did
Kristin: it's actually equal with what you are giving up vs. what i get monetarily
Kristin: and you can't eat while you are there
Kristin: food is not included
Kristin: are you smiling yet?
Ms. Sake: my turn yet?
Kristin: yes
Ms. Sake: k
Ms. Sake: i would never think it is about money with you
Ms. Sake: EVER
Ms. Sake: i get that
Ms. Sake: however
Kristin: what's the issue
Ms. Sake: if you can get a great deal on a hotel and airfare
Ms. Sake: that is my gift

Ms. Sake: i'm salaried dear
Ms. Sake: time off, time on, doesn't matter
Ms. Sake: I get equal pay when i am away
Kristin: but it costs you vacation time
Kristin: you get 2 weeks paid vacation
Ms. Sake: so it's not about money for me either
Kristin: then what gives?
Ms. Sake: no, i get more than that
Ms. Sake: i want this to be a shared experience
Ms. Sake: down the line
Kristin: fine, you pay for what you eat?
Ms. Sake: we share EVERYTHING
Kristin: i gave in a little but no more
Kristin: not one bit
Ms. Sake: time, money, feelings, touching
Kristin: so we are on?
Ms. Sake: to a shared experience - absolutely
Kristin: i liked the intimacy conversation better
Ms. Sake: come here - i want to kiss you
Kristin: i am right next to you
Ms. Sake: not the same
Kristin: that is correct
Kristin: i'm listening to the song
Kristin: i love it
Ms. Sake: i know
Ms. Sake: and I can't tell you how much that tells me
Kristin: i love it:)
Ms. Sake: about you
Kristin: does that really surprise you?
Ms. Sake: i went to my car and brought it inside at work
Kristin: i'm actually really sensitive
Ms. Sake: and i listened to it through your ears
Kristin: ultra
Kristin: and what did you hear?
Ms. Sake: i know why i liked it
Kristin: because we are similar
Kristin: it's very scary yet so where you want to be
Ms. Sake: there is this rhythm to it
Kristin: falling in
Kristin: and yes the rhythm is so me
Kristin: all of it
Kristin: the beat
Kristin: very sensual
Ms. Sake: i remember the words mostly

85

Kristin: meaningful
Kristin: yes you do
Kristin: i remember the feelings
Kristin: shocker
Ms. Sake: it resonated
Kristin: me too
Kristin: remember last night
Ms. Sake: it's something that goes to your very core
Kristin: i said something about famine or feast
Ms. Sake: i can't forget it - and don't want to
Kristin: i thought it was a different song of hers but it was this one
Ms. Sake: yes, i remember
Kristin: and you shouldn't it's powerful
Kristin: it's the core
Ms. Sake: is that your favorite line?
Kristin: nope
Ms. Sake: what is
Kristin: take a breath and count to 10
Kristin: i knew you would ask
Kristin: that's the falling for me
Kristin: b/c i wouldn't if i wasn't there
Kristin: the rest is a given
Ms. Sake: mine is there's a silver moon
Ms. Sake: that your heart can't waste
Kristin: the silver moon starts the same rhythm
Ms. Sake: and then suddenly
Ms. Sake: there's a stranger's kiss that you
Ms. Sake: can't wait to taste
Kristin: taste like an apple
Kristin: you have a great memory
Kristin: is in site you take a bite
Ms. Sake: we all struggle to belong
Kristin: hoping everything that is wrong will be alright
Kristin: yes
Ms. Sake: That was weird!!!
Kristin: why
Kristin: we are on the same page
Kristin: when will you learn
Kristin: you try again
Ms. Sake: i wrote the line that was just before yours
Kristin: until you get it right
Ms. Sake: hoping that
Kristin: of course you did, does that surprise you?
Kristin: really, i will show you

Ms. Sake: yes
Kristin: when it's right and good it's good
Kristin: nothing more, it's not difficult
Ms. Sake: come on kristin
Ms. Sake: did you share a similarity with all the other women
Kristin: no
Kristin: never
Kristin: but i knew it existed
Ms. Sake: remember, it's feast or famine
Kristin: never have i felt this
Ms. Sake: that's one of your favorite lines
Kristin: it's great
Kristin: nope
Ms. Sake: true
Kristin: i just learned it from this song that you shared with me
Kristin: here's me
Ms. Sake: but it resonates
Ms. Sake: that means it belongs to your core
Kristin: i never doubted beliefs
Kristin: or wants
Ms. Sake: that's why you recognize it
Kristin: hadn't found it but knew it was out there
Ms. Sake: but you've wanted before
Kristin: it does belong to my core
Kristin: wanted yes, found it no
Kristin: but knew it was out there
Ms. Sake: you've orchestrated before
Ms. Sake: you've paid before
Kristin: but never got for what i paid for
Ms. Sake: you've gone the extra mile
Kristin: nope
Kristin: it just is
Ms. Sake: made the effort
Kristin: no
Kristin: timing and fate
Ms. Sake: struggled to belong
Kristin: we all do
Ms. Sake: hoping everything would be alright
Kristin: everybody has this right to these feelings and expectations
Kristin: did i say the expectation word, yes i did
Kristin: i expected to find this
Kristin: and i wanted to find this
Ms. Sake: see the difference?
Kristin: yes i learned it from you actually

Kristin: thank you
Ms. Sake: what is your core?
Kristin: i want to love and be loved unconditionally
Kristin: that is my core
Kristin: hence my passion for animals
Kristin: you see i know what i want
Kristin: and what i like
Kristin: most do not but i do
Kristin: and i won't settle
Kristin: ever
Ms. Sake: unconditional love isn't right
Kristin: never have, never will
Ms. Sake: that's why you won't settle
Ms. Sake: you've given that
Kristin: who's?
Ms. Sake: and not received it in return
Kristin: how
Kristin: doesn't mean that i don't want that
Kristin: and i never gave up hope for that
Kristin: lady gave me that
Kristin: so i did get that
Ms. Sake: unconditional is different from magical
Kristin: one way or another
Ms. Sake: yes, but lady depends on you for her survival
Kristin: don't break my bubble
Kristin: lol
Ms. Sake: you don't ever want a partner to be like that
Ms. Sake: that's too much pressure
Kristin: no it's not
Ms. Sake: that means you are the world to each other
Ms. Sake: and that's not right
Kristin: no it doesn't
Ms. Sake: k
Kristin: it means that you expect nothing
Ms. Sake: i'm listening
Kristin: but you get unconditional love
Kristin: they love you for just being you
Ms. Sake: you really didn't just type that?!?
Kristin: you don't have to do anything
Kristin: yes i did
Ms. Sake: didn't we have this discussion already
Kristin: no
Kristin: you can have your life
Ms. Sake: the difference between expecting and wanting

Kristin: get things from others
Kristin: it doesn't mean that you don't get unconditional love from friends as well
Ms. Sake: don't you believe that you should expect?
Kristin: it's not about one person giving you everything
Kristin: that is stupid
Kristin: yes i expect things from my friends, family and lover
Ms. Sake: it's not unconditional...its honest
Kristin: that's incorrect
Ms. Sake: i would expect my friends to be conditional
Kristin: k_____ would love you unconditionally
Ms. Sake: 'Listen, Donald...'
Kristin: even if you murdered somebody and you were sitting in jail
Ms. Sake: 'I love you, but your hair has got to go!!'
Kristin: she would visit you
Kristin: be mad as hell at you
Ms. Sake: not so
Kristin: you would tell her why you did what you did
Kristin: and she would believe you
Ms. Sake: not so
Kristin: really?
Ms. Sake: Really
Kristin: what if it was for a good reason?
Ms. Sake: there is no good reason
Kristin: she wouldn't trust you until proven otherwise?
Kristin: really, self defense?
Ms. Sake: except self defense
Kristin: doesn't count
Kristin: mind reader
Kristin: listen to my example
Kristin: you fight everything
Kristin: she would give you the benefit of the doubt because she knows you
Kristin: until proven otherwise
Kristin: unconditional
Ms. Sake: nope
Ms. Sake: and i wouldn't expect her to
Ms. Sake: she would protect herself
Ms. Sake: and stay away from the crazy people
Kristin: i would expect my friends to trust what they know about me
Kristin: and they know that i would NEVER do that unless provoked
Kristin: self defense
Ms. Sake: and if in some convoluted world i thought murder was acceptable and did it
Ms. Sake: she would know i wasn't right

Kristin: knew subject
Kristin: new
Ms. Sake: UNCONDITIONAL love only happens one time
Kristin: nope
Kristin: don't say
Kristin: it
Ms. Sake: (aside from children and animals)
Kristin: parent child
Ms. Sake: damn you
Kristin: i disagree
Ms. Sake: stop it
Ms. Sake: don't read my mind
Kristin: it's not true
Ms. Sake: for one minute
Kristin: i'm good at that, when will you learn
Kristin: i get what you are about to say
Ms. Sake: your confusing terminology
Kristin: but you are speaking to the wrong person
Ms. Sake: it's never unconditional after you get burned once
Kristin: if i had a child, yes i would agree with what you are about to explain
Ms. Sake: every person who walks into your life after that has a bar to meet
Kristin: but i've been on the other side and that is not true for everybody
Ms. Sake: a standard to achieve
Ms. Sake: me too darling
Kristin: so give me your everybody UNCONDITIONAL advice
Ms. Sake: and the result has been disappointing
Kristin: not necessarily, i have learned
Ms. Sake: yes, i believe you have
Kristin: i don't trust the parent child paternal bond
Kristin: it doesn't exist for everybody
Ms. Sake: and i trust that for you unconditional is the state you want to be
         in
Kristin: that much i have learned
Ms. Sake: and i too want that
Ms. Sake: so let's agree on something
Kristin: no, that state is where you lay your head at night
Kristin: unconditional is different
Kristin: my motto growing up was 'home is where you lay your head at
         night'
Kristin: unconditional is different
Kristin: i must be clear on that as that is my core
Ms. Sake: it's where you hang your heart
Kristin: true, hate you for that, lol, yes but true
Ms. Sake: i know

Kristin: haven't heard that before, same thing i guess
Kristin: unconditional is when you expect NOTHING
Kristin: in return
Ms. Sake: i agree
Kristin: can we agree on that?
Kristin: k
Kristin: so what is unconditional love to you?
Ms. Sake: i know that i don't have to expect anything from you because your core dictates that you will always deliver
Ms. Sake: and you don't stray from your core
Ms. Sake: like me
Kristin: true
Ms. Sake: unconditional is more dependant on one's survival
Ms. Sake: you must depend on me to live
Kristin: i disagree
Ms. Sake: but that's only good for pets and kids
Ms. Sake: because it makes sense
Kristin: i won't see that ever
Ms. Sake: k
Ms. Sake: then i won' t try to make you
Kristin: i see what you are trying to say but i disagree
Kristin: that's okay
Ms. Sake: got it
Ms. Sake: yes it is
Ms. Sake: and i love that you have that opinion
Ms. Sake: and want to stick to it
Kristin: i do
Kristin: it is what it is
Ms. Sake: i won't try and make you move
Ms. Sake: i don't even want to
Ms. Sake: true
Kristin: you shouldn't and won't
Kristin: that's normal, i think
Ms. Sake: so tell me more about how you miss me
Kristin: smiling here, i really do
Ms. Sake: same here
Kristin: i wish i were in bed with you right now
Ms. Sake: me too
Kristin: holding each other
Ms. Sake: touching each other
Kristin: it's comforting and something to look forward to
Ms. Sake: listening to each other
Kristin: yes
Ms. Sake: listening for those marks

Kristin: yes
Ms. Sake: those tell tale signs
Kristin: touching, breathing
Kristin: that's what it is all about
Ms. Sake: that let you know you are moving
Kristin: losing time
Ms. Sake: the outline of your face against the light
Kristin: you are too kind
Ms. Sake: your hair cascading down around your face
Kristin: but i can say the same thing
Ms. Sake: and that timing
Kristin: your body pressing against mine
Ms. Sake: saying the right thing at the right time
Kristin: it's all about timing
Kristin: well, i'm not so good at that
Ms. Sake: just a little, but always enough
Ms. Sake: just enough
Kristin: my actions speak better than words
Ms. Sake: to make me ask for more
Kristin: b/c i feel with my hands
Ms. Sake: or feel
Kristin: i see that
Ms. Sake: with that
Kristin: feeling is everything
Ms. Sake: i'm sending you to bed
Ms. Sake: as i must be too
Kristin: you are sending you to bed
Kristin: good night
Ms. Sake: meeting in the morning
Kristin: i'm off to write
Kristin: write
Ms. Sake: honey, it's late
Kristin: yes meetings for both of us
Kristin: i don't sleep
Kristin: but sweet dreams to you
Ms. Sake: we'll work on that
Ms. Sake: you need rest
Kristin: yes we will
Ms. Sake: we all do
Kristin: yes i do but my mind races
Kristin: good night
Kristin: sweet dreams
Kristin: don't answer what i wrote
Ms. Sake: how does Wednesday sound?

Kristin: PERFECT
Ms. Sake: you come here
Kristin: i thought you would never ask
Kristin: yes
Ms. Sake: or i can come there
Kristin: nope
Ms. Sake: it doesn't matter
Ms. Sake: i love your place
Kristin: lady and i will come to you
Ms. Sake: and it's pretty close to work
Kristin: nope
Kristin: lady and i will be there
Ms. Sake: Wednesday it is
Kristin: yes it is
Ms. Sake: until then...
Kristin: good night, you need to work on aruba dates as i have some changes to make
Kristin: sweet dreams
Ms. Sake: you are there now...so they are always sweet
Kristin: good, as you are
Kristin: funny how life works out, it really is
Ms. Sake: stop it, you made my flutter
Kristin: nite
Kristin: good
Ms. Sake: not funny
Ms. Sake: nice to know
Ms. Sake: that it does pay off
Kristin: it wasn't meant to be funny
Kristin: sincere
Ms. Sake: i know
Ms. Sake: true
Kristin: sweet dreams
Ms. Sake: i was thinking about that
Ms. Sake: you and i are meant to be
Kristin: now sign off, i'm not responding anymore:)
Ms. Sake: k
Ms. Sake: bye
Kristin: yes
Kristin: bye"

It was 1:45 a.m. and I was trying to finish this chapter, as I will never be able to sleep again. I am signed off from the Internet for the first time, writing this, listening to her CD, feeling things I have never felt before, and about to retire to bed. I love her and she loves me unconditionally, even though she doesn't believe in that word, as it equates to pain for her; but I do. It is what it is and since I am the author, I can write the unconditional word and pay the wrath for it at a later date.

One has to love differences in people. When one's heart is connected in all senses of the word, do the differences really matter? Nope, as long as you are both on the same page what does it really matter? That's the beauty of love. It's such a wonderful feeling to finally come home for the first time. To feel completely connected with life and another person; wanting to share everything with her and others. I wanted nothing more than to share these feeling with others, as I am the happiest I have ever been in my entire life and all of this was possible through Internet dating.

CHAPTER 24

Today was another "real date" with Ms. Sake. We have not slept with one another yet; we are still taking things slowly so as to not create false intimacy.

Lady and I drove to her house and we had decided to attend another festival. This would be interesting, as we had not yet found a "festival." We entered and shared a passionate kiss as she finished getting dressed for the day. She couldn't make a decision on what to wear; the heat was unbearable, and after several outfit changes, she ended up in a sexy pair of jeans and a tight stylish tank top, looking mighty fine. I didn't comment on the outfit; I was shy and we were headed out the door.

She drove us to Laguna Beach. We were several miles from her house when she said, "So, do you like the outfit or should we go back and I can change?"

I immediately said, "No, you look fabulous."

She smiled and said, "Good." I'm feeling like an ass for not saying something at her house but I didn't want to sound forward. Note to self: comment on sexy outfits as I see them.

We were driving to the festival, reminiscing about our last non-festival outing. But we were confident that we would find this festival, as it's the largest and best-known festival in Laguna Beach. We found parking, fed the meters with seven hours of parking, and walked along the beach, laughing and looking for the festival.

Doesn't it figure that we couldn't find It? We both started to panic on the inside, but not really, because who could lose this festival? We walked for a while; she finally asked a lifeguard for directions, and we headed off in the correct direction. We walked and walked and walked, and now we were both hesitant, as there was clearly no festival in sight. Finally we turned the corner, and lo and behold, we were at the entrance to the festival. We took a deep sigh, paid our entrance fee, and enjoyed what was about to unfold.

We walked around, talking about the different mediums for several hours, ate lunch, then finally settled in with a few glasses of wine and listened to the musicians. Before we knew it, we lost ourselves in each other, soaking up the sun; her shoes were off, feet resting on my chair. My body was slightly draped over her calves and we were laughing, not a care about what was going on around us. Suddenly she leaned over and said, "Do you notice that we were draped all over each other and neither one of us cared?"

I smiled, glanced around, and said, "Yes, itsn't it wonderful?" We were both happy. At that moment, it didn't matter that we were lesbians, openly flirting in a heterosexual environment without a care in the world. We sat for another hour enjoying each other and the conversation, when we decided that we both wanted to go back to her house. We gathered our belongings. She stated that she was cold and I commented that I wasn't surprised, in that she was barely wearing anything. I was not jealous; that was a genuine comment coming from me, and she understood. She smiled and we left!

We walked back to her car laughing and talking, when suddenly she pulled me into a covered parking garage. We started kissing and making out. We had a wonderful moment. I was a bit nervous but feeling good with where we were at. About 15 minutes later, we emerged back onto the sidewalk, continuing our walk back to her car. We found the car, got in, and before I knew it, she was on my lap. We were kissing and making out. We both wanted nothing more than to bang each other's brains out, but we pulled ourselves together and made the long, painful drive back to her house. We sang songs, talked, held hands, and made our way back to her house.

This was another wonderful Sunday for both of us, as we have now spent the past several Sundays together and we always ended the evening watching *Sex and the City,* after which I made my way back to Los Angeles. We returned to her house, snuggled up in her bed fully clothed, and caught the last five minutes of *Sex and the City*. Neither one of us wanted this evening to end, and as our show was ending, we both immediately showed a great interest in the next show, *Project Greenlight.* She gave me the brief rundown, we snuggled back into each other's arms again, and before I knew it, we are all over each other, trying to behave ourselves, again basically having sex with our clothes on. She asked me to spend the evening. I told her that I needed to go back to Los Angeles, as the traffic would be a lot less this time of the evening, rather than rush hour traffic. But I got her to snuggle back into my chest for another ten minutes. Finally she said that I must go. I reluctantly agreed, gathered Lady, had another long passionate kiss at the door. We peeled each other off of each other and I left.

How we got out of there without sleeping with one another is something neither of us will understand, but it is what it is. The week was about to start again, and we looked forward to our flirtatious e-mails, longing for one another. "Wow" is all I can say; never have I experienced this kind of energy or connection before, and I long for when we are together next.

CHAPTER 25

Somewhere throughout Tuesday, we both worked and e-mailed back and forth. She sent me the cutest pictures of five kitties that were about to go to the pound and she decided that we were going to save one of them. She asked me which one would I keep? I scrolled through the photos and immediately saw the cutest gray fur ball; I immediately said this one and his name would be Sylvester, as I was convinced that it was a boy. She didn't hesitate for one moment, researched my questions, found out that it was a little girl, and agreed to keep her. She was to come home Wednesday evening.

We both were thrilled with the first addition to our family. We agreed to get together Wednesday evening. The evening ended with our usual I.M.; funny how this has transpired, we met in person, worked together on and off for one year, yet got reunited through e-mail, and this seems to be our preferred method of communication. The following I.M. transpired, apparently she was watching the rerun of *Sex and the City*, the episode that we caught only the last five minutes of our last evening together:

"*Kristin: he breaks up with her on a post-it*
Kristin: she and Mr. big will end the season together
Ms. Sake: wait
Kristin: b/c it was out of character for that to happen
Ms. Sake: i see them still together
Ms. Sake: burger and her
Ms. Sake: uh oh
Kristin: keep watching honey
Kristin: he hurts her in a messed up way
Ms. Sake: she just woke up alone
Kristin: leads her on
Ms. Sake: yes...this we saw
Kristin: oh, you missed the previous part, we both did
Kristin: apparently
Kristin: they broke up
Kristin: he was to walk away and think about things
Ms. Sake: i like our version better
Ms. Sake: what was that again?
Kristin: he came back into her apartment and said this is what i want, you
Ms. Sake: lots of hugging and kissing
Kristin: and then left the post it

Kristin: i like our version much better
Kristin: as the melissa ethridge song says 'this is gonna hurt like hell'
Ms. Sake: stop
Kristin: stopped
Ms. Sake: so
Kristin: what?
Ms. Sake: tell me
Kristin: i listen to all of your music
Kristin: yes, what?
Ms. Sake: in looking back on the e-mail
Kristin: and?
Ms. Sake: when did i have you?
Kristin: the message in the bottle
Kristin: but honestly when i first met you
Kristin: there was a strong curiosity and attraction
Kristin: couldn't put my finger on it but something stirred me
Ms. Sake: isn't that MY line?
Kristin: nope
Kristin: just the truth
Kristin: sister told me not to go there
Kristin: during our first work event
Kristin: so i didn't
Kristin: i didn't say anything
Kristin: but was very curious
Ms. Sake: well, curiosity ended
Ms. Sake: my friends have requested the pleasure of meeting you
Kristin: our excursion to san diego was awesome
Ms. Sake: i told them we would come up for air after a while
Kristin: i'm sure they have and i am happy to meet them
Ms. Sake: and then we will accommodate
Kristin: i would love to meet them
Kristin: yes this weekend i figured that would happen
Ms. Sake: nope
Kristin: k
Kristin: when you let me know then that is the time
Ms. Sake: i am remaining selfish for a while and want you all to myself
Kristin: i love that
Ms. Sake: they will have plenty of time
Kristin: yes they will
Kristin: whatever you want i am here
Ms. Sake: they're great people
Kristin: i'm not going anywhere
Ms. Sake: and there are only a few
Kristin: of course they are

Ms. Sake: i don't have a huge base of friends
Ms. Sake: just a handful of really close ones
Kristin: that's what is important
Ms. Sake: there's not enough time to be spread out
Kristin: you have met my closest of friends
Kristin: exactly
Kristin: i'm blessed with that
Ms. Sake: good.
Kristin: so what else is on your mind?
Kristin: i have you for a few more minutes as you unwind
Ms. Sake: k
Ms. Sake: i'm getting closer to agreeing to fall in
Kristin: shoot the moon
Ms. Sake: into aruba
Kristin: i love to hear that
Kristin: LOVE
Ms. Sake: not quite there yet
Kristin: as i have never expected you not to be
Kristin: k
Ms. Sake: and i want you to know something
Ms. Sake: it's not about control
Ms. Sake: really
Kristin: i understand
Kristin: say no more
Ms. Sake: k
Kristin: i want you to be comfortable
Kristin: that's all that i want
Ms. Sake: you make it hard not to be
Kristin: and whatever that is, makes me happy
Kristin: it's not meant to be hard
Kristin: i want you to take the time off from work
Kristin: show up
Kristin: and have an incredible time as you will
Kristin: we will
Kristin: that's all i want
Ms. Sake: you know what else?
Kristin: no pressure just fun
Kristin: what?
Ms. Sake: isn't it
Ms. Sake: wonderful
Ms. Sake: how connected we can be
Kristin: more than i ever could imagine
Ms. Sake: even though we aren't in each other's presence
Ms. Sake: k

Kristin: absolutely, incredible
Ms. Sake: i hear you
Kristin: i love it, are you kidding me?
Ms. Sake: i'm not sure
Ms. Sake: i know how i'm feeling
Kristin: i get that it's weird how friends one day and over time feelings change everything
Kristin: everything
Kristin: i know how i am feeling and we are on the same page
Ms. Sake: so you actually believe that this is the one?
Kristin: i do
Kristin: want to read a chapter or two to tell you?
Kristin: not now but later
Ms. Sake: you believe this because you want to or because it has revealed itself?
Kristin: i have never felt the way that i do
Kristin: i know that
Kristin: and i believe in love
Kristin: lasting love not short term flings
Ms. Sake: but you have had these very intense relationships
Kristin: as you have
Ms. Sake: and i remember thinking how, in the beginning
Kristin: we aren't different
Kristin: yes in the beginning it can create false intimacy
Ms. Sake: how there might not be enough drama for you to stay interested
Kristin: i don't need or want drama, as you don't
Kristin: we both know that
Ms. Sake: yes, i know that now
Ms. Sake: that's part of the fascination
Kristin: it's not drama that draws me to you
Kristin: it's you that i like
Kristin: if i were to die tonight i would be in bliss
Kristin: that much i can say
Ms. Sake: see that's what scares me
Kristin: and for the first time i can rattle off a zillion things that i like about you
Kristin: why does that scare you?
Ms. Sake: that's what i would say
Kristin: i think it's awesome
Ms. Sake: and i am used to being the one who believes
Kristin: not anymore
Ms. Sake: true
Ms. Sake: thank god
Ms. Sake: thank you

Kristin: i could never say that before
Kristin: your welcome
Kristin: before it was forced
Kristin: i tried, yes and it worked for a while
Ms. Sake: exactly
Kristin: but not for long
Kristin: this is different
Kristin: and i don't have to explain to anybody
Kristin: i love that
Kristin: people see that i am happy
Ms. Sake: so do i
Kristin: and not trying to show them the reasons why
Ms. Sake: me too
Kristin: it just is
Kristin: and i laugh
Kristin: i'm happy
Kristin: even when i'm not with you
Kristin: but because of what we share
Kristin: absolutely
Ms. Sake: there's this unique strength
Kristin: and if it were to disappear i would fight forever for that
Kristin: i never had in the past
Ms. Sake: that shows through every move i make now
Kristin: didn't have a care or need or interest too
Ms. Sake: there's a confidence
Ms. Sake: that was never available to me
Kristin: there should be with both of us
Kristin: we have been honest with each other
Kristin: from the beginning, we are who we are, no pretenses
Ms. Sake: i can't wait to see you
Kristin: me neither
Ms. Sake: i can't wait to hold you
Kristin: i am calm for the first time in my life
Kristin: i can't wait to breathe in your breath
Kristin: that's what it's all about
Ms. Sake: that is the sweetest thing anybody has ever said
Ms. Sake: to me
Kristin: trusting that feeling and going with it
Kristin: it's true
Ms. Sake: i feel complete - i am always calm
Kristin: i am usually restless but no more
Kristin: people around me see my calmness
Ms. Sake: and i have this sense of being safe
Kristin: as you should and i do too

Kristin: and i haven't before
Kristin: i can't explain other than i feel more alive than ever
Kristin: in all aspects of my life
Ms. Sake: that is so awesome
Ms. Sake: how lucky are we?
Kristin: we are
Kristin: and i can express it openly
Kristin: not scared one bit
Kristin: or forced one bit
Kristin: and again i have never felt this way before
Kristin: i love it
Ms. Sake: me too
Ms. Sake: you are something
Kristin: i know b/c we communicate with each very well
Kristin: and we are honest and don't hold back
Kristin: we lay it on the line
Kristin: why wouldn't we, it feels great
Kristin: you are something
Kristin: i have my faults, you have your faults, that's human nature
Ms. Sake: and i can't wait for that one awkward moment when you walk in
        the door and we want to hold each other and kiss so badly that we
        stumble through small talk to get to into each other's arms
Kristin: no small talk honey
Ms. Sake: you know what i mean
Ms. Sake: the pleasantries
Kristin: yes i do, that's what lady is for
Kristin: she just barges in
Ms. Sake: now sylvester
Kristin: i love that
Kristin: i know, are you sure you like that name?
Kristin: now that it is a girl
Kristin: i told the girls about sylvester
Ms. Sake: 'honey look - sylvester is clinging to lady's back
Kristin: i love that name
Kristin: and lady won't mind one bit
Kristin: she's really good about kitties
Ms. Sake: you say that know
Ms. Sake: now
Kristin: i know
Ms. Sake: k
Kristin: she loves what i love
Kristin: it's all good, i promise
Ms. Sake: oh, so you love sylvester already?
Kristin: can you tell?

Ms. Sake: yeah
Ms. Sake: you don't hold back
Kristin: i don't, why?
Kristin: when you feel it you feel it
Ms. Sake: true
Kristin: she will be a lap kitty
Ms. Sake: k
Ms. Sake: that'll be different
Ms. Sake: for me
Kristin: i have my work cut out for me
Kristin: i know
Kristin: you will like it and brandy (her other cat) will still have her place
Kristin: the only place in your heart
Kristin: and the others fit around that spot
Kristin: that's the key to getting a lap kitty
Kristin: and keeping a luv-er
Ms. Sake: ahhh
Ms. Sake: you should write a book
Kristin: that's the truth
Kristin: brandy doesn't have a thing to worry about
Kristin: there is always room for others
Kristin: just not losing site of her in the process
Ms. Sake: and then there is that special place...
Kristin: of course
Ms. Sake: meant for only a few
Kristin: yes
Kristin: there is lots of room
Ms. Sake: and if you're lucky enough...
Kristin: it's amazing what the heart can hold
Kristin: and forget
Kristin: and give
Ms. Sake: true
Kristin: it's a forgiving instrument
Kristin: and very accepting
Kristin: and before you know it your in love
Ms. Sake: it's in your best interest to do so
Kristin: but of course It is
Kristin: for myself and others
Ms. Sake: forgive and learn
Kristin: i hear ya
Ms. Sake: and love again
Kristin: of course
Kristin: take the chance
Ms. Sake: so, i was thinking about something

Kristin: what have you got to lose, be happy
Kristin: yes?
Ms. Sake: about your aruba proposal
Kristin: yes
Ms. Sake: about the making love there...
Kristin: yes
Ms. Sake: and i was wondering if we could hold out till then
Kristin: yes
Ms. Sake: think about that anticipation!!!!
Kristin: tomorrow was not the night
Kristin: if we can make it through the weekend then i agree to aruba
Kristin: the ball is in your court
Kristin: whatever you want, i am game
Kristin: but i can't wait for tomorrow
Ms. Sake: i know i can't make it that long
Kristin: but not for that, it was never about that
Ms. Sake: it would have to be a concerted effort
Kristin: i'll try my best if that is what you really want?
Ms. Sake: and then i think about how long that is
Kristin: it's a long time honey
Kristin: but i'm game if you are
Ms. Sake: and how i keep saying i can take it slow
Kristin: i hear you
Ms. Sake: and the next thing you know i'm all over you
Kristin: but
Ms. Sake: but i do want it to be special
Kristin: it's a great thing
Kristin: it will be special
Ms. Sake: yes
Kristin: no matter what
Ms. Sake: that i know
Ms. Sake: for sure
Kristin: and it will happen when it's supposed too
Ms. Sake: i just thought it would be extremely romantic
Kristin: i hear ya
Ms. Sake: but not very practical
Kristin: but you said something the other evening that i could never answer
Kristin: and that was
Kristin: what would be different if we made love sunday evening vs. the future?
Kristin: i couldn't answer that and i still can not
Kristin: because honestly nothing
Kristin: other than we get to know one another more
Ms. Sake: true

Kristin: but we are already there

Ms. Sake: and we'd just be missing out on all that lovemaking

Ms. Sake: you're right

Kristin: so, it will happen when it happens unless you want to wait

Ms. Sake: it's not something we are capable of anyway

Kristin: i'm good with that but that doesn't have anything to do with how i feel about you

Ms. Sake: i can't wait

Kristin: me either

Kristin: we already know what the experience will be like

Ms. Sake: okay...that sent a shiver through my body

Kristin: we were there saturday

Kristin: it's true

Kristin: we were totally connected

Kristin: and will be

Kristin: it's all good, it really is, that's why i don't need that

Kristin: to be complete

Ms. Sake: sorry...i went there mentally for a minute...

Kristin: we have that already...good, as you should

Ms. Sake: i went back to saturday

Kristin: i understand

Kristin: i've been there many of times

Ms. Sake: there isn't a close enough

Kristin: there never will be

Kristin: that i promise

Kristin: and i don't promise much

Kristin: as you have learned

Ms. Sake: i need to clear my mind

Ms. Sake: i need to let go, don't i?

Ms. Sake: i'm holding onto perceptions

Kristin: your fine just the way you are

Ms. Sake: no

Kristin: those will fade away with time

Ms. Sake: you think this is good

Kristin: i can only be me

Kristin: you can only be you

Ms. Sake: but it only gets better

Kristin: it is what it is

Ms. Sake: and it only goes to that level that few experience if i let go

Kristin: of course it gets better because of how we feel

Kristin: we already know that

Ms. Sake: shiver

Kristin: you don't have to let anything go, it just melts away

Ms. Sake: no, i do

Kristin: no forcing what so ever
Kristin: really you don't, it will melt away
Kristin: it has too, it just does
Kristin: we have all been hurt
Kristin: we all have protective gear on
Ms. Sake: i haven't
Ms. Sake: i've made sure of that
Kristin: but the right key to the door opens everything
Ms. Sake: i've built my life so as not to get hurt
Kristin: but the right key
Ms. Sake: remember
Kristin: it all goes away
Ms. Sake: i was the unseen
Ms. Sake: stop
Ms. Sake: i constructed my life so as to remain that way
Ms. Sake: i was hurt as a child
Ms. Sake: i was not loved enough
Ms. Sake: so i went through life
Ms. Sake: making sure
Ms. Sake: the love i received was enough
Ms. Sake: it took a lot of bullshitting on my part
Ms. Sake: a lot of convincing myself that i was in love
Ms. Sake: a lot of rationalization
Ms. Sake: my hurt
Ms. Sake: my pain
Ms. Sake: stems from not believing
Ms. Sake: hold on...
Ms. Sake: as long as i didn't believe...then there wasn't anything that could hurt me
Ms. Sake: i never felt safe as a child
Ms. Sake: i remember thinking my father would die or go away and we would be stranded
Ms. Sake: we were European and there wasn't an abundance of love
Ms. Sake: i was 30 something before i heard those words from my own mother!!
Ms. Sake: so i overcompensated in my relationships
Ms. Sake: i became the perfect girlfriend
Ms. Sake: everything I would want in a lover
Ms. Sake: usually wasted
Ms. Sake: on someone who didn't get me or didn't have enough soul to understand
Ms. Sake: and that was fine
Ms. Sake: i learned how to be a great partner
Ms. Sake: and now you come along

Ms. Sake: at a very interesting time in my life
Ms. Sake: when everything is coming together
Ms. Sake: coming together not in a tangible sense
Ms. Sake: but in an essence
Ms. Sake: i can feel my own power and strength
Ms. Sake: coming to life and making a difference
Ms. Sake: and i need someone who can relate
Ms. Sake: relate
Ms. Sake: and someone who also has that power
Ms. Sake: power
Ms. Sake: you
Ms. Sake: you can be that
Ms. Sake: you have that quality
Ms. Sake: that essence
Ms. Sake: you can shake the very core of me
Ms. Sake: and i have spent oh so many nights
Ms. Sake: protecting that core
Ms. Sake: but lately
Ms. Sake: i've found that the core is not what i thought it was
Ms. Sake: its about coming home
Ms. Sake: returning to who i really am
Ms. Sake: tearing down the facade
Ms. Sake: i built to protect myself from the pain of being a child who
couldn't get enough attention
Ms. Sake: and yearned for it
Ms. Sake: that's why I was in band and drama and held down a full-time job
since i was 15
Ms. Sake: and went around and washed cars and delivered newspapers and
worked at the cafeteria
Ms. Sake: and bought all my own clothes and cars and supplies
Ms. Sake: and was as independent as a child could be
Ms. Sake: i never wanted to depend on anybody...
Ms. Sake: - pause -
Kristin: what has shaken your core is the fact that we have shown each
other the belief that we never thought existed?
Kristin: what we protected
Kristin: our entire lives and that is what is shaking the core
Ms. Sake: more than that
Kristin: and
Ms. Sake: if i build a dream
Kristin: allowed each other to be ourselves
Ms. Sake: and keep it just out of reach
Ms. Sake: hold on
Ms. Sake: if i build a dream and keep it just out of reach

Kristin: but when you touch it, it's inviting correct?
Ms. Sake: then i will never be disappointed
Kristin: you want more
Kristin: you taste it and want it
Ms. Sake: because it will always remain a dream
Kristin: again, the key to the door that one never thought was real
Ms. Sake: that thing that you strive for
Kristin: but then the right key opens that door
Ms. Sake: yes
Kristin: and you are left standing there wondering
Kristin: looking
Kristin: think it's a dream
Kristin: but you know it's real
Kristin: but you question it
Kristin: think "what the hell have i been thinking?"
Kristin: this entire time because i feel so wonderful right now
Kristin: u question it
Kristin: want to hide from it
Kristin: but then you wonder
Kristin: hmmm, this feels good
Kristin: really good
Ms. Sake: i question it because when you make a dream a reality, you shatter the myth
Kristin: do i trust it
Kristin: do i go with it or ruin it
Ms. Sake: stop
Kristin: like old patterns have shown me
Kristin: but this time it feels a lot different
Kristin: therefore shakes the core
Kristin: makes you wonder
Kristin: question reality
Kristin: vs. dreams
Kristin: and you make a decision
Kristin: do you go for it, stop it or ruin it
Kristin: the choice is yours
Ms. Sake: no
Kristin: that's the beauty of it all
Ms. Sake: i know you are for real
Ms. Sake: do you get the magnitude for me?
Kristin: but you have to trust that i get you and that i get me, at the same time
Kristin: i really do, trust me on this one
Kristin: one really knows
Ms. Sake: do you see that you were born in some child's dream?

Kristin: you fall in
Ms. Sake: where love was a unicorn?
Kristin: i sure hope so
Ms. Sake: something only fairytales were made of?
Kristin: nothing better and it's revealing itself now
Kristin: maybe
Ms. Sake: you weren't supposed to be real
Kristin: i don't know anymore
Kristin: but i am real
Ms. Sake: you say you are
Ms. Sake: you want to believe too
Ms. Sake: only time will tell
Kristin: time will only tell
Ms. Sake: the honeymoon will fade
Kristin: so you fight it or go with it
Ms. Sake: and you'll be left with the details of a life struggle
Kristin: you have no choice at this point really, you will be hurt either way
Kristin: your in it
Ms. Sake: will you feel the same?
Kristin: as i am in it
Kristin: i do
Kristin: clearly read what i have written
Kristin: i'm not afraid of it
Ms. Sake: then
Kristin: i have never felt it
Ms. Sake: i won't be either
Kristin: i have always wanted it
Kristin: and now that i am here i embrace it
Kristin: i don't fight it
Ms. Sake: i will give unto you everything
Kristin: i don't want to
Kristin: i know you will, as i will
Kristin: i feel it
Kristin: i love it
Kristin: it's great, i couldn't ask for anything more
Ms. Sake: you are a dream deferred and now realized
Kristin: it's hard to trust in something that you can't touch
Kristin: good, then go with it
Ms. Sake: no...it's hard to trust in something that wasn't suppose to exist
Kristin: but i do exist
Ms. Sake: you were the carrot
Kristin: and i'm not sorry for that
Kristin: now you have the carrot, enjoy it
Ms. Sake: the thing i was supposed to struggle to get

Ms. Sake: but the carrot always comes before the cart
Kristin: you did struggle
Kristin: not with me
Ms. Sake: you aren't actually supposed to get the carrot - ever
Kristin: it's all about timing honey
Ms. Sake: that's the point
Ms. Sake: true
Kristin: that's the point
Ms. Sake: SO
Ms. Sake: enough
Ms. Sake: i will fall in
Ms. Sake: and go to aruba
Kristin: i hope so, we are already there
Kristin: aruba is the carrot
Ms. Sake: and make mad, passionate love to you when the time comes
Kristin: yes, i concur
Ms. Sake: and revel in your being
Ms. Sake: and soak in your flavor
Kristin: and i get to kiss you tomorrow
Kristin: what more could i ask for
Ms. Sake: and make you happy to be alive!!!!!!!!
Kristin: you do that already, one can't remove my grin
Kristin: ever
Ms. Sake: yes
Ms. Sake: i concur
Kristin: i thought so
Ms. Sake: i certainly have a sense of serenity
Ms. Sake: about me these days
Kristin: as i do, it's peaceful for once
Ms. Sake: and my smiles are all related to thoughts of you
Kristin: we enhance each others lives
Kristin: that's what it's all about
Kristin: remember how sister and i are on the same path with relationships?
Kristin: funny how that has happened
Ms. Sake: yes...
Kristin: and the comparison couldn't be any stronger
Kristin: strange but true
Kristin: i spoke to her about that this morning
Ms. Sake: i thought so
Kristin: and she agreed
Ms. Sake: it's good to be all of us...
Ms. Sake: honey...
Kristin: yes it is
Ms. Sake: i don't want to end this

Kristin: i know, bed time
Ms. Sake: but...
Kristin: i hear you
Kristin: sweet dreams
Ms. Sake: i still have to finish that proposal
Kristin: as i will have you in my presence tomorrow evening
Ms. Sake: true
Kristin: and i can't wait
Kristin: and so it is
Ms. Sake: ohhhhh my...i can't wait to see you!!!!!!
Ms. Sake: and lady of course
Kristin: me neither
Ms. Sake: get some rest and eat some wheaties
Kristin: i can't think of anything better, honestly
Ms. Sake: sylvester shall be here in the morn
Kristin: yes she will and i can't wait
Ms. Sake: xxo
Kristin: you too honey"

So another I.M. ended our evening and we can't wait to see each other. I took a chance and sent her a chapter of the book, the one where we spent Saturday in bed at my house. I think it would be interesting for her to read about our experience from my point of view, and I'm willing to take that chance as I feel completely comfortable where we are. She has shown an interest in my writing, so I attached the chapter, hit the send button and I'm done with it. Who would have thought that e-mails, I.M.'s, and personal contact could bring such joy? Only time will tell, but we certainly are on the right path to happiness.

CHAPTER 26

Today is Wednesday. We are breaking the rules as I am going to spend the evening on a school night and meet Sylvester for the first time. I am so excited, I can't stand myself. I left work. Lady and I drove to her house. We walked in the front door; I immediately kissed all over her as to not let her think that I was only there to meet Sylvester. We embraced, kissed, hugged, then I glanced over and I saw the sweetest angel sleeping on the end of the couch. I was immediately drawn to her. I picked her up. She cried and wanted nothing to do with me. I put her down. My feelings were hurt, but not really, as she had only been in her new house for less than one hour.

Ms. Sake was cooking us dinner. We flirted. We hung out and played with the kitty. We ate our meal, babysat; the kitty fell asleep and we had our alone time. We stayed up until 4 a.m. making out. We were still on our best behavior as we were waiting two more months for our upcoming Aruba trip to make love for the first time. I doubt that will happen but we get an "A" for effort. I drifted off to sleep with the little kitty nestled in my hair. I woke with a kitty scarf wrapped around my neck. She had accepted me. I slept for two more hours and Ms. Sake was awake the entire night. I left early, as I had a long commute ahead of me. Again it was the best evening a girl could ever hope for. We definitely have a connection and now we have an addition to our family, and we are both excited about this.

I worked all day. I returned home, exhausted, walked through the front door at 7:30 p.m. and crashed for the entire evening. We e-mailed a bit throughout the next day but not too much, as we both were busy. We knew that we were getting together Saturday; we both had to work at her casino in the evening for our upcoming event. We were both looking forward to working together. She really has to work; I offered so I could be with her, get to see her office, and steal a kiss on her couch. I loved working under these circumstances. Thursday evening arrived and we started I.M.'ing the following:

"*Kristin: hey, what's the name of that janet jackson song?*
Kristin: how rude of me, hello lovely
Kristin: then my question
Kristin: O:-)
Ms. Sake: ...hello - it's sooo good to see you on...
Ms. Sake: which janet song are you talking about?

Ms. Sake: the one on my tape?
Kristin: absolutely
Kristin: whatcha doing?
Ms. Sake: just stepped into my office for a breather...
Ms. Sake: and it smells so lovely in here
Ms. Sake: thanks to the wonderful lilies...
Kristin: i'm glad you like
Ms. Sake: what's not to like?
Ms. Sake: water you doing?
Kristin: nothing really
Ms. Sake: finished the laundry?
Kristin: everything is great
Kristin: i decided against the laundry and decided to write
Kristin: changing your name in the book, any suggestions?
Ms. Sake: i've grown fond of sake
Kristin: i don't like ms. sake and that will take a lot or re-editing
Kristin: it feels wrong
Kristin: mad
Ms. Sake: because it was a depiction of the weapon of mass destruction that leveled me for a day and a half
Ms. Sake: clearly indicating i cannot hold my sake?
Kristin: well, now you are changing my mind
Ms. Sake: is that why?
Ms. Sake: (half)
Kristin: no from a readers point of view it sounds weird
Ms. Sake: well
Ms. Sake: explain it then
Kristin: i like ms. beach
Ms. Sake: sake came to your mind for a reason
Kristin: b/c of your fateful evening
Ms. Sake: actually, Ms. Festival is more descriptive
Kristin: b/c i knew what you were doing without being there
Ms. Sake: or, ms. non festival
Kristin: nope
Ms. Sake: someone else holding that title?
Kristin: neither
Ms. Sake: k
Kristin: they are cities or job titles
Kristin: only 100 or so
Kristin: so you are not limited
Kristin: shoot for the moon and you might get a star
Ms. Sake: true
Ms. Sake: count to ten and you might fall again
Kristin: hold your breath

Ms. Sake: take a chance?
Kristin: like your heart will probably break
Kristin: but you can't seem to leave that thing alone
Kristin: and your scared to death
Kristin: and fall in love again
Kristin: and everything that looks wrong will be all right
Kristin: you swear you keep romance at a distance
Kristin: but it's always famine or feast
Kristin: and a hungry heart forgets
Kristin: but minimizes regrets
Kristin: there is a silver moon
Kristin: and your heart races
Kristin: do i know this song?
Ms. Sake: and a strangers kiss you cant wait to taste
Kristin: okay i'll stop, your turn
Kristin: maybe this time you will give a little more
Ms. Sake: so in the middle of the night
Ms. Sake: he'll hold you tight
Kristin: and find somebody who isn't as crazy as the times before
Kristin: so you try again
Kristin: and hold on tight
Ms. Sake: and then suddenly everything will be all right
Kristin: exactly
Ms. Sake: i must be on a different verse
Kristin: you got the ending
Ms. Sake: so, is everything all right?
Kristin: yes, i love this song, THANK YOU
Kristin: and for you being just you
Kristin: it's all very good
Kristin: and just right
Ms. Sake: ms right
Kristin: i couldn't ask for anything more
Kristin: i like it, that's for book # 2
Kristin: that will be all about you
Kristin: i hope you don't mind
Ms. Sake: nope
Kristin: see i'm on the ending of this book and i want the second to be
about the one
Kristin: i love the idea
Kristin: i know, i'm crazy
Ms. Sake: why would you say that?
Kristin: most think i'm crazy
Ms. Sake: i think we can make an interesting enough life for enough
material for a whole series of books for you

Kristin: see, we are on the same page
Kristin: good
Ms. Sake: whatever you want...
Kristin: i'm going to quote you on that... ha
Ms. Sake: don't ever give up on your dreams and ambitions
Kristin: i never will
Ms. Sake: you know as well as i that everything that means anything springs from them
Kristin: absolutely
Ms. Sake: I'm just happy that you can finish this book now and move on to the next chapter...that's fabulous
Kristin: i'm done, i need your chapter
Ms. Sake: and I am interrupting that process
Ms. Sake: you're done?!?
Kristin: although you are a much better writer, so if you end it you will need to write the next one
Kristin: b/c the readers will love the last chapter
Ms. Sake: then it would be your book
Kristin: it's all my book with you honey
Ms. Sake: maybe a collaborative effort...
Kristin: but of course
Kristin: but you are really the better writer
Ms. Sake: i only wanted the last chapter to give you a break
Kristin: i'm just crazy enough to take the chance
Kristin: and write about this kind of stuff
Ms. Sake: and to show you what the last chapter looks like through someone else's eye's
Kristin: see, now you are thinking
Kristin: i will make you write it and enjoy every moment
Ms. Sake: some of the world's GREATEST books will never be published because they have never been written because people don't take chances like you
Ms. Sake: so there
Ms. Sake: besides...the last chapter is already written...i just need to format it and we both wrote it
Kristin: i agree but it's also good to write it all down
Kristin: don't you enjoy reading about our experience?
Kristin: something exciting and great about that
Ms. Sake: absolutely
Ms. Sake: and to see it from your view is fascinating
Kristin: i'm sure
Ms. Sake: to say the least
Kristin: i am the author
Kristin: i can say whatever i want to, right?

Kristin: it's all fiction, correct?

Kristin: r i g h t

Ms. Sake: it's like this...

Ms. Sake: we may both see a color and assume we are both seeing the same shade of orange, let's say

Ms. Sake: but in reality we are both seeing different hues and nuances

Ms. Sake: so when I read your chapter of me

Ms. Sake: i was very drawn to what was going through your mind

Ms. Sake: because i can't read yours when i am with you

Ms. Sake: i'm too busy trying to kiss you

Ms. Sake: so it's very romantic to see it down on paper

Ms. Sake: and to tell you the truth

Ms. Sake: it was a little hard for me

Ms. Sake: it's rough to read someone's caring in print

Ms. Sake: I wanted to go to where ever you were and hold you or kiss you or send you a gift

Ms. Sake: but noooo...i had to sit there and see it in writing right in front of my face

Ms. Sake: and take it in

Ms. Sake: and after i read it the second time...i did just that

Ms. Sake: i actually closed my eyes

Ms. Sake: and let it wash over me

Ms. Sake: (i didn't think to count to 10)

Ms. Sake: i felt it

Ms. Sake: and it almost made me cry

Kristin: really?

Kristin: i was scared to share

Kristin: i didn't want to scare you or make you mad

Ms. Sake: you can't scare me

Kristin: you can scare yourself

Ms. Sake: and i promise never to be mad and not talk it through with you

Ms. Sake: i'm sure we can work through anything

Kristin: that's what i was afraid of

Kristin: what was hard for you to read?

Kristin: because i almost sent you several other chapters but didn't

Kristin: i took it slow and you only got one

Kristin: it's not easy to put myself out there like that

Ms. Sake: the part about taking yourself off of the market

Ms. Sake: it was what i wanted

Kristin: that was in the beginning

Ms. Sake: that was hard too

Kristin: i understand

Kristin: but that was the truth

Ms. Sake: i didn't know it until i read it though

Kristin: but i understand because you wouldn't know

Kristin: that's the hard part about reading what my feelings are, i mean the book

Kristin: and you wouldn't know

Kristin: it must have been exhilarating in one sense to hear that not from me personally

Kristin: and to see how my mind unraveled from my point of view

Kristin: that's the part that was scary on my end

Kristin: but not scary for me because that is how i feel

Ms. Sake: i know...i appreciate you taking that chance and exposing yourself - so to speak

Kristin: i share in one way or another

Ms. Sake: the truly worthwhile stuff is supposed to be scary

Kristin: i'm just so used in being told that i have to SPEAK how i feel

Ms. Sake: i know

Kristin: and i don't like that

Ms. Sake: i love the way we communicate

Kristin: me too

Ms. Sake: we do it on with so much different media

Kristin: communication is in many forms

Kristin: mind reader

Ms. Sake: when we are together we can or don't have to share

Kristin: sharing is good

Ms. Sake: or we can do it this way...which is much more safe for both of us

Kristin: i can't get away with only e-mailing

Kristin: talking is good and i do that

Kristin: i'm not good at it but okay

Kristin: you are much better

Kristin: it just is

Ms. Sake: i wasn't always a talker

Ms. Sake: i'm just curious

Ms. Sake: and that requires asking

Kristin: nothing wrong with that but don't hold that against me

Kristin: because i trust where you are

Ms. Sake: i prefer e-mailing myself

Kristin: and I don't need a lot of questions for me to get where you are

Ms. Sake: and I. M. ing

Kristin: it doesn't mean that i don't care

Ms. Sake: i talk all damn day long

Kristin: I.M.'ing or talking

Kristin: i don't need a bunch of questions to get where you are

Kristin: you share

Ms. Sake: hold on

Ms. Sake: gotta go for a sec

Kristin: in all means... okay... work beckons
Kristin: i know you are busy, sorry for you but i just sent you another
chapter of which i haven't edited."

I'm on a roll with sharing my feelings, no holds barred and it is what it is. I e-mailed her chapter 23, scared to death because I sent her the "unconditional love" chapter which she detests but it is what it is and that is how I feel. I retired for the evening, knowing that I will see her in one more day.

CHAPTER 27

Friday arrived. We were to see each other tomorrow evening. I was excited to see her and the kitty "Sylvia," as she has renamed her without asking me. That is fine with me; the name fits her well. Throughout the week, she has sent me flowers twice. I love them and they are beautiful. I had planned to send her flowers today and I do so anyway. The following I.M. transpired:

"*Ms. Sake: August will be much better - that's a promise!! Thanks for the flowers - they are gorgeous!! xxoo*
Kristin: that i know, i'm happy they made it
Kristin: i made my local place drive out to you since i had to work:)
Ms. Sake: Now is it my turn to say, 'You shouldn't have?!?'
Ms. Sake: but of course I am glad you did
Kristin: i hope so
Kristin: now you can enjoy the lovely comments:)
Ms. Sake: that's the easy part, 'They're from someone I care deeply about, thanks for asking!'
Ms. Sake: gotta run - yet another counseling session..."

We e-mailed throughout the day. I came home, wrote, went to bed, and woke with the anticipation of a fabulous date with Ms. Sake and Sylvia. I puttered throughout the day. Went to work, gathered our filming equipment, and headed to her casino for filming and to see her. Lady, of course, came with me. We arrived at the casino. I unloaded our camera equipment, carried Lady into Ms. Sake's office, where she was no where to be found. I got Lady settled in and headed off to meet our producer for filming. Before he showed up, I ran into her coming out of her office as I went to check on Lady. It was cute, as she had just noticed Lady, she got her settled again and was shutting the door off to find me when I startled her in a pleasant way. We went back into her office and shared pleasantries. She finally locked the door and we were able to kiss, hug, and greet each other in an appropriate manner that only she and I understood. It was sweet; then the phones started ringing and we were both off working!

We worked for a few hours on and off, flirting and having a great time. I was stuck in the ballroom and she was nowhere to be found. I was tired of working, missing her; I was really not working, just hanging out, helping our producer, and wanting to see her. Finally I am over it all and I text messaged her, as we were supposed to have dinner and it was already 8 p.m. I text messaged her the following:

"r u getting hungry? Come save me. So and so just kissed me, YUCK, let's meet in your office, you tell me what time?"

Thankfully, within several minutes, Ms. Sake appeared and saved me. I was hiding on stage with the tournament director when she came and saved me. He jokingly said "You cannot take her away, she is keeping me company." He was cute, but thankfully we disappeared into a back alley and headed off to dinner.

I followed her to the restaurant. We ordered, made small talk; she asked me if I was nervous and to be honest, I was nervous because I wanted to touch her and I knew I couldn't. It made things a bit uncomfortable as we were there on business, and that felt odd yet comfortable. We had a good meal, then headed back to her office as it was time for Lady to be walked. We made out on her couch until somebody knocked on the door, knocking us back to reality; then we agreed that I would go back to her house and wait for her. I would take care of Sylvia. She walked me to my car. She handed me her house key, and Lady and I were off to wait for her.

We drove to her house, walked in, and I immediately searched for Sylvia. She would have none of that. I went to the fridge to grab a beer and to begin my search for the missing kitty, when I discovered that Ms. Sake had stocked the fridge with my favorite beer. There was a note wrapped in a black ribbon around one of the bottles, saying "Just you wait until I get home." I couldn't wait, to be honest. I wished she was there at that very moment, but I had to wait, dammit. It took me 45 minutes to find Sylvia and three phone calls to Ms. Sake. I found no humor in a missing kitty in somebody else's house!

Sylvia finally appeared. Ms. Sake showed up ten minutes later. We immediately kissed, played with Sylvia, and finally fell asleep at 6 a.m. We had to call the casino at 5:30 a.m. to remind them to remove a camera and put it in Ms. Sake's office for safekeeping.

We woke at 11 a.m., rolled around, fooled around, finally prying ourselves off of each other, as we needed to be productive this Sunday afternoon. Her house needed a little attention paid to it since she had spent the last month persuing me. The least we could do is pay attention to her needs and her house's needs.

We spent the day shopping at Home Depot. We replaced an electrical outlet, installed a wine cooler, repotted all of her flower pots, cleaned out the Jacuzzi. I hadn't even realized that she had a Jacuzzi in the privacy of her back yard. We had a wonderful day. We went to the store, picked up wine to stock the wine cellar, and then we had a lobster dinner and watched our normal *Sex and the City*. We immediately started fooling around, she lit candles; this evening was going to be the evening that we first made love, we both just knew it. We settled in. She had the Jacuzzi warming up all afternoon and finally said to me "Let's go in the Jacuzzi." She started rummaging for bathing suits, and she said to me, "Do you want a one-piece or a two-piece?"

I responded with, "Neither, I want naked."

She immediately dropped all the suits, walked over to me, and said, "Are you being serious or are you kidding?"

I said "I never kid about that. Naked." She was happy and grabbed us each robes and we headed outside.

We slipped into the Jacuzzi naked for the first time. We snuggled up to one another and made out for over one hour before deciding that we couldn't take it anymore and went into her bedroom. We closed up shop and headed inside. She returned to bed in the sexiest outfit I have ever seen —tank top and short, sexy football shorts. She looked amazing. She actually looked amazing in the Jacuzzi. I wanted to tell her a handful of times how pretty she looked, but I thought that would sound stupid so I held back. I wished I hadn't, because she looked delectable. We snuggled into the bed, both relaxed from the Jacuzzi, and we fell asleep around 1:00 a.m. We woke at 5:00 a.m. and made love for the first time. She started kissing me. I was more than accepting, as I had wanted this the previous evening, but she had fallen asleep.

It was amazing. We spent several hours making love before I had to peel myself away and head back to her casino to pick up the camera and go to work. I hated leaving her in that bed; I wanted nothing more than to hold her all afternoon, but I dressed, packed up, and Lady and I left.

She had her work day, I had my work day. She leaves in a few days to go out of town this weekend. We were scheduled to see each other Wednesday evening before she left.

We were in love; both of us had fallen and we were enjoying every moment of it. Though we had not said the words to each other yet, we both felt it. She has read the last several chapters of this book; however, no words have been spoken yet.

CHAPTER 28

The work week dragged on and we wanted nothing more than to see each other.

Wednesday evening; this would be our last evening until Sunday, as she was going out of town. We had a date planned and both of us were to leave work at 6 p.m. At 5:57 p.m., Lady and I were driving to her house. She was caught up at work. We stopped by the pet store to pick up a few items, as Sylvia would be spending the weekend at my house. I needed to gather kitty items to make her current stay and future stays as comfortable as possible.

We made it to her house and somehow, she had beaten us home. Lady and I walked in. We immediately smiled, hugged, kissed, and snuggled into each other. We could barely pry ourselves off of each other to decide what we wanted to do for the evening. At this rate, we weren't going to get anything accomplished other than ourselves, which wasn't such a bad option to either of us.

We decided that we were hungry and that we wanted to rent a movie. We jumped into her car, headed to the grocery and movie store. The grocery store was fun, because we were able to shop and flirt at the same time. Like a beat was never missed, yet enticing at the same time. We are still learning what each other likes and doesn't like. She is learning that I always pick the slowest line in the grocery store. I learn that she likes to shop in bulk and buy more than she will ever eat because she is getting a "deal" at that very moment on whatever item is on sale. She learns that I don't like any spices. I learn that she loves spices; therefore, we will always have two separate dishes when we cook—mild and hot. She learns that grocery stores will steam lobsters for you. I learn that her favorite wine is Cake Bread. Who would have thought that such a chore could be so enjoyable!

We then proceeded to the video store, picked our movie, and headed back home. She cooked up an amazing meal. We ate in the living room, finished eating, played with the kitty, and then played with each other. We were like two high school kids making out on the couch, laughing, giggling, cuddling, petting, kissing. An hour later, we decided to move into the bedroom, as we had a movie to watch. It was already midnight and this was another school night. We snuggled in, watched the movie, laughed, talked, and tried to figure out the ending of the movie. It was lovely, to say the least.

Then we start fooling around, listening to music, getting our groove on, still fully clothed but too comfortable to change or to get naked. Besides, we are still taking things slowly and enjoying each other. People make a mistake: after they first sleep together, then every time afterwards they immediately get naked and forget that romance still exists. We listened to music, changed CD after CD, and finally dozed off around 4:00 a.m., listening to Dr. Hook.

We both awoke at 6:00 a.m. We decided that we couldn't keep our hands off of each other, so we indulged in what we wanted to partake in the previous evening. It's 9 a.m., and I'm supposed to be on the road. Sylvia is spending the weekend at my house. I needed to get her settled in, be at work by 9:30 a.m., and I am one hour from home. But the moment had finally happened and there was no going back.

I insisted that her clothes be removed. She agreed and we spent the next hour enjoying each other to the fullest. It was amazing is all that I can say. It was 10 a.m., Sylvia and I must leave, as I am now in the dog house. Sad part is, we could have stayed doing what we were doing for many more hours; we were just getting started. But finally, Lady, Sylvia, and I hit the road.

We raced home. I dropped Sylvia off. I arrived at work at 10:40 a.m., one hour late. It was not pretty, but well worth the wrath that I had to pay. Better planning next time will be necessary.

We hardly e-mailed throughout the day, as we both had a ton of work to do. She was leaving this evening for a weekend in San Francisco with some friends. After a few e-mails, the following I.M. transpires before she hits the road over one hour late:

"Ms. *Sake: U there?!?*
Ms. Sake:: k, I'm leaving now to get on the road...
Ms. Sake: and drive...for a long time...to Valencia
Ms. Sake: just me and the radio, as i have no CD player...
Ms. Sake: going along...singing a song
Kristin: hey
Ms. Sake: till I get static
Ms. Sake: excuse me
Kristin: i was trying to send u a photo of sylvia sleeping
Ms. Sake: i'm having a conversation with myself - do you mind?

Kristin: but i can't get my video camera / camera to download it properly
Ms. Sake: ahh
Kristin: i've been video taping her for you
Ms. Sake: stop teasing me
Kristin: she fell and u would be proud, i didn't help her
Kristin: bad mother
Kristin::)
Ms. Sake: hooray
Kristin: u will see
Ms. Sake: you have learned the ways of the dark side
Ms. Sake: you must now feel the force
Kristin: i don't like it but she is your cat
Ms. Sake: it surrounds you
Kristin: well mine too but i respect what u say
Ms. Sake: honey, she is OUR cat
Kristin: i know
Ms. Sake: she stays at my house
Kristin: but u have discipline with her and i do not
Kristin: so i listen and respect your rules
Ms. Sake: u r wrong
Kristin: as i have none
Ms. Sake: you do have discipline
Kristin: gasp, i'm never wrong
Ms. Sake: as you just said you didn't help her
Ms. Sake: after she fell
Kristin: i know, i know
Ms. Sake: was there much blood
Ms. Sake:???
Kristin: mere flesh wound
Kristin: just a pint
Ms. Sake: and why didn't you help her?
Ms. Sake: am I that cruel
Ms. Sake:???
Kristin: more than you can donate at a blood mobile
Ms. Sake: elephant
Kristin: no, she was fine, it was actually cute
Kristin: k u
Kristin: go
Ms. Sake: no
Kristin: i don't want u on the road at all hours
Kristin: this evening
Ms. Sake: no
Kristin: what?
Ms. Sake: NO

Ms. Sake: i'm not going
Kristin: what do u want?
Ms. Sake: it isn't obvious yet?
Kristin: no
Kristin: apparently not...smiling here
Ms. Sake: i haven't had enough
Ms. Sake: i haven't had enough of you
Ms. Sake: not yet
Kristin: you're cute
Ms. Sake: don't let go just yet
Kristin: was the closure of your evening good?
Ms. Sake: let me say something
Kristin: go ahead
Ms. Sake: one never knows what can happen on trips
Kristin: yes
Ms. Sake: and you don't want to leave someone you care for behind
Ms. Sake: without letting them know what they mean to you
Ms. Sake: and i know you know
Kristin: honey i know
Ms. Sake: so stop typing
Kristin: as you know
Ms. Sake: now
Ms. Sake: sit on your hands
Ms. Sake: anyway
Ms. Sake: what i was going to say
Ms. Sake: that you probably didn't know
Ms. Sake: was that I feel such a kinship with you
Ms. Sake: you are something special
Ms. Sake: and every so often i look at you
Ms. Sake: and i wonder why you are standing next to me
Ms. Sake: not in a bad way
Ms. Sake: but we've already discussed
Ms. Sake: that others have wanted this spot
Ms. Sake: have given up things for this spot
Ms. Sake: and i am moved to
Ms. Sake: appreciate this chance
Ms. Sake: right here...right now
Ms. Sake: to make everything all right
Ms. Sake: because...in
Ms. Sake: hold on someone walked in
Kristin: k
Kristin: i did very well listening and i will wait for you to return, finish and
tell me when it's my turn

Kristin: we have a connection and we are standing together because this spot is our spot

Kristin: and nobody else's spot, therefore, what others have given up would suffice

Kristin: i know somebody there, i will stop

Kristin: i will share a secret with you, you can read when this person leaves

Kristin: remember the psychic i was telling u about who records stuff

Kristin: anyway from the beginning he always said that i was special, different and actually put on this earth for a reason

Kristin: not your normal reasons either, it's hard to explain i will need to find the tape

Kristin: but he always said that i was here to teach people things

Kristin: people come in and out of my life for things that i teach them

Kristin: i'm not even aware what i am teaching some of the times

Kristin: but my energy is just that, they get what they want and they move on

Kristin: some get caught in the allure and want more but all learn something, grow and move forward

Kristin: kind of like a spiritual healer, it's great but it's lonely b/c people draw from me and leave

Kristin: but with you i am getting what i am giving for the first time and that is awesome

Kristin: baby you need to leave, no more, let's pick up sunday evening...safe travels...xoxox

Ms. Sake: NO

Ms. Sake: i'm not finished

Ms. Sake: but I'll tie it up now

Ms. Sake: you

Kristin: k

Ms. Sake: and me

Ms. Sake: is a dream come true

Ms. Sake: you've heard it before

Ms. Sake: but i want to say it again

Ms. Sake: you hit on it a little

Kristin: ?

Ms. Sake: you said something about feeling alive

Ms. Sake: more alive than ever

Kristin: why am i different?

Ms. Sake: more confident

Ms. Sake: more powerful

Kristin: to u

Ms. Sake: i can walk around now feeling my power and strength

Ms. Sake: you are different to me because

Ms. Sake: you fulfilled that one special thing

Ms. Sake: that i didn't think existed
Kristin: but u always had
Ms. Sake: that i spent many days talking about in therapy and
Ms. Sake: with friends
Ms. Sake: no
Ms. Sake: not what i had
Ms. Sake: what you accepted
Ms. Sake: we talked a little
Ms. Sake: about me
Ms. Sake: needing to feel appreciated
Ms. Sake: by doing
Ms. Sake: not by existing
Ms. Sake: you said right away
Ms. Sake: that you didn't want me to do anything
Ms. Sake: that really hit home
Ms. Sake: it was the space I was looking for
Ms. Sake: to crawl into and make mine
Ms. Sake: and you continue to do so
Ms. Sake: you make me feel special because you think i am special not because i do more or spend more or talk more or act more...
Ms. Sake: and i don't NEED you, I WANT you
Ms. Sake: that's the biggest difference
Ms. Sake: i want to enjoy you
Ms. Sake: and i do
Ms. Sake: i don't need to fix you
Ms. Sake: or teach you
Ms. Sake: or be a role model
Ms. Sake: i can really enjoy you for who you are
Ms. Sake: because you are something special too
Ms. Sake: okay
Ms. Sake: i'm done
Ms. Sake: i've bothered you enough
Ms. Sake: i've interrupted your time
Kristin: you have not bothered me at all
Ms. Sake: with sylvia
Kristin: stop
Ms. Sake: and i have to go
Kristin: you are correct
Ms. Sake: i'm so very late
Kristin: yes u r
Kristin: but i get to say one thing
Ms. Sake: i'll miss u
Ms. Sake: k
Kristin: i enjoy you as much as you enjoy me

Kristin: and
Ms. Sake: not on line
Ms. Sake: in person
Kristin: k
Ms. Sake: wait
Ms. Sake: it's enough to know
Ms. Sake: in our hearts
Ms. Sake: and share
Ms. Sake: when we are in front of each other
Ms. Sake: but i get it and you
Ms. Sake: and i'll take you with me on this trip
Ms. Sake: and forever
Ms. Sake: wherever
Ms. Sake: so I'm off
*Kristin: k, just remember your two fingers on your heart and you are good
        to go*
Kristin: goodnight and safe travels
Ms. Sake: got it
Kristin: i know u do b/c u do it to me
Kristin: goodnight
Ms. Sake: nite nite"

How cute is she? She thought I was going to say that I loved her over the Internet. Silly girl, as if I would ever do that, not so much as that moment will be an in person moment. She is off to San Francisco. I placed an order of flowers for her for a Monday morning arrival at work declaring my love for her as I know we will say the words Sunday evening. I am left with the animals and a wonderful weekend to write and just be me. Isn't love grand!

CHAPTER 29

Ms. Sake was in San Francisco and I was in Los Angeles. We text messaged a few times. I was doing my thing, she was doing her thing; unusual for lesbians, as they are normally up each other's asses, but not us. Space is healthy and friendships are great. I spent Friday evening writing. I woke Saturday morning, ran my errands, stopped by her house to water the plants and feed Brandy, when I came across this amazing sexual note that she left me:

"hello sweetheart!
Happy Saturday (or Sunday morning?!?)
I miss you...
I've dreamt about coming home and walking up to you and grabbing you and deep kissing you...then I'll hold you tight as we wrap around each other-another we start rocking to our own internal beat that is driving our breathing harder...longer...louder...etc"

You get the point; I leave out about ten chapters of what she wrote. *Ahhh,* is all I have to say. I wished she were standing in front of me as I was reading this but she is not.

I went home. My friend came over for the evening. We had a great evening, talking, reminiscing about our great relationships, as both of our girlfriends were out of town at the moment. People forget the importance about sharing great moments in relationships with friends, reliving those acts of kindness and the feelings associated with them. It solidifies the relationship, actually, allows it to breathe and just be. I enjoyed doing that for the first time in awhile, enjoyed the evening with my friend. She left shortly after midnight. I fell asleep, as I was exhausted and excited for the following evening with Ms. Sake upon her arrival back into town.

She returned home. Sylvia, Lady, and I drove to meet her at her house. We walked into her house. I unpacked the kitty and observed her happiness at returning home. Ms. Sake and I fell immediately into where we last left off. We can't keep our lips, hands, hugs, and breaths off of each other. All we do is hug and drink each other in. It's hard to explain, it is just where we both wanted to be. We putzed around. I cooked a meal, because I wanted to show her that I could cook, but it was late. We weren't hungry but I did it anyway. We retired to the bedroom with no food in our bellies, as neither of us was hungry. We ended up kissing and holding each other throughout the evening.

There was a moment when she was lying on top of me, she looked at me and she said, "Say it."

I said, "What, you already know that I love you."

She sweetly said, "I love you too." We kissed for about 30 minutes and she said, "Say it."

I gently laughed, enjoying every moment of what was transpiring, and I said, "Baby, I love you, I have for quite some time."

She smiled, nestled into my chest, and exclaimed, "Thank God I can now say it as much as I have wanted to. I will say it a lot. I hope you like that."

I responded with "I sure hope so."

At 3 a.m. we finally fell asleep. We woke at 6 a.m. We kissed, fooled around, and drank each other in before I left for work. She left for work, and our days were off and running.

It was perfect, and the funniest part is that I knew this was going to transpire. I had previously ordered flowers on Saturday to be delivered to her work for a Monday delivery saying the following:

"I am thankful for you sharing your life with me on a daily basis, I love you"

I knew that we were going to exchange the words Sunday evening, as this was important for her to hear. Not I, per se, as I knew the feelings were there long ago, but I respected what she needed to hear. I professed my love with the words and a follow-up reinforcement in the form of a flower arrangement.

Monday afternoon arrived, and so did the arrangement of flowers for Ms. Sake. It consisted of red roses at the base of the arrangement for my love for her, irises as the stem of our growing friendship and the strength that will get us through the tough times, and white roses at the top of the arrangement with the hopes, romance, and anticipation of our future. I loved her and I wanted her to know it.

132

She and I e-mailed back and forth throughout the day. We were talking about work mainly, but also a few personal things, before she finally received the flowers and our ongoing I.M. from the day picked up at that point:

"*Kristin: didn't i once say to you that you don't want to go falling in love with me because of my writing?*
Kristin: ha
Ms. Sake: ha ha
Ms. Sake: you know that is the way to my heart
Kristin: i can't find that e-mail, dammit
Kristin: but of course i did honey
Ms. Sake: now tell me
Ms. Sake: what
Ms. Sake: was supposed to come out of last night
Ms. Sake: that you knew you were supposed to be there?
Ms. Sake: aside from the obvious
Ms. Sake: or is there an aside?
Kristin: it will all become clear soon
Kristin: and then i will disclose
Ms. Sake: another surprise?!?
Ms. Sake: you certainly are interesting Kristin
Ms. Sake: I really like that about you
Kristin: something that was done before today, that is all i can say
Ms. Sake: and of course you know it absolutely pushes me out of my comfort zone
Kristin: good
Ms. Sake: keeps me on my toes
Kristin: nothing wrong with that
Ms. Sake: and always keeps me wanting to be more
Ms. Sake: better
Ms. Sake: for you
Ms. Sake: too bad I'm too tired to do that properly
Kristin: wanting is good
Kristin: not the case
Ms. Sake: yes
Ms. Sake: sometimes
Ms. Sake: I must say
Ms. Sake: you are making some impact
Kristin: i like that, as you are
Ms. Sake: that's a good thing
Kristin: it's a great thing
Ms. Sake: true
Ms. Sake: now go

Ms. Sake: as I must
Ms. Sake: :(
Kristin: u r releasing me this time
Kristin: for now
Ms. Sake: true
Ms. Sake: only for now
Kristin: check back in later
Ms. Sake: ciao bella

Time passes

Kristin: hey are you there?
Kristin: i keep bugging you...
Ms. Sake: Okay you...
Ms. Sake: I just got THE most gorgeous arrangement of flowers!!!
Ms. Sake: YOU are too much!
Kristin: oh good i'm happy they arrived
Kristin: they better be red roses and iris
Kristin: and white roses as they were out of white tulips
Ms. Sake: sorry...somebody walked in
Ms. Sake: Yes - beautiful irises and red & white roses
Ms. Sake: everyone is shocked when they see your bouquets
Ms. Sake: you are quite a catch!! People are jealous of ME!
Ms. Sake: You have now raised the bar!!
Ms. Sake: Are you listening to my phone message?!?
Kristin: was that you that called?
Ms. Sake: yes
Kristin: i will when we are finished here
Ms. Sake: thought I would break the record
Kristin: that place does a great job with flowers
Ms. Sake: hold on
Kristin: k
Kristin: brb, i'm happy they arrived and that you like them
Ms. Sake: YOU do a great job!
Ms. Sake: I don't know what I did to deserve these and you, but I'm sure
        grateful for whatever it was and that you came into my life...
Ms. Sake: i love you too, babe
Kristin: your too cute
Kristin: i did have these ordered saturday
Kristin: so trust me i was going to see you last evening no matter what time
        you came home:)
Ms. Sake: ahhhh...now the plot is revealed
Ms. Sake: ulterior motives
Kristin: no plot

Ms. Sake: i like it
Kristin: not really
Kristin: just is
Ms. Sake: i know
Kristin: r u being productive today?
Ms. Sake: we both knew we were going to right
Ms. Sake: hold on
Kristin: i'll finish what you were writing and then back to work—right when
you returned from san fran as we almost did the last evening that
we were together ...we've felt it for awhile, we have never been shy
about that...
Kristin: k u...more later...
Ms. Sake: cu

Pause

Ms. Sake: Hello?????
Ms. Sake:
Ms. Sake:
Ms. Sake:
Ms. Sake: Okay...I've calmed down
Ms. Sake:
Ms. Sake:
Ms. Sake:
Ms. Sake:
Ms. Sake:
Ms. Sake:
Ms. Sake:
Kristin: no need to calm down...
Ms. Sake: you're back...
Kristin: i'm back
Ms. Sake: how was your day dear?
Kristin: it was good, how was your day?
Ms. Sake: It was productive
Ms. Sake: very

Work stuff transpires, as we do work together...

Ms. Sake: you busy?!?
Kristin: yes it should
Ms. Sake: am i bothering you
Kristin: i got a lot done and i have a more to do
Kristin: not one bit
Kristin: i'm leaving soon

Ms. Sake: good for you
Kristin: i'm done working mentally
Kristin: work wise
Ms. Sake: and where are you mentally?
Kristin: with you
Ms. Sake: need i ask
Kristin: us
Kristin: nope
Ms. Sake: same here
Ms. Sake: and now for my confession...
Kristin: yes
Ms. Sake: aside from the obvious - i love you.
Ms. Sake: i have a cold
Ms. Sake: (did i mention i love you?)
Kristin: yes you did
Ms. Sake: so if you don't feel well
Ms. Sake: you can hurt me later
Kristin: i don't catch colds
Ms. Sake: just wait till i feel better
Kristin: i take ziacam
Kristin: don't worry, i hope you feel better
Ms. Sake: there isn't a cure for the cold
Kristin: it prevents colds
Ms. Sake: what's ziacam
Kristin: that's why i didn't offer you any ziacam because u have a cold
Kristin: i'll introduce it to you
Ms. Sake: i see
Ms. Sake: i'll let you get back to work, you fabulous woman!
Ms. Sake: ciao
Kristin: i hope you feel better...bye you i'm not working anymore tonight as i
        am heading home shortly:)
Ms. Sake: okay...then I'll continue to talk
Ms. Sake: write
Ms. Sake: type
Ms. Sake: you can keep me company
Ms. Sake: i wasn't into work any more either
Kristin: you have me for 7 minutes and then i am walking out the door
Ms. Sake: k
Kristin: do u know the meaning of irises?
Kristin: red roses?
Ms. Sake: i know red roses
Kristin: and white tulips but you ended up with white roses as they were
        out?
Ms. Sake: and white roses

Ms. Sake: explain irises...

Kristin: red roses are the base of the boutique as that is for our love

Ms. Sake: yes...love and friendship are at the base

Ms. Sake: that's a good start

Kristin: irises are a sweet flower with sentiments of affection, grace & solitary!!!!...

Kristin: they mean hope, affection, grace, beauty, power, faith, wisdom and valor

Kristin: white roses are silence and that i am worthy of u and that u are heavenly

Kristin: so the red roses are the base, the stem is the iris's and the top are the white roses

Kristin: tulips are romantic flowers in general, signifying a perfect love, abundance...i love tulips

Ms. Sake: it's beautiful...just like you!

Ms. Sake: there's a lot of meaning in this pot

Ms. Sake: i love it

Kristin: that's actually why i was upset when i saw the other flowers last time even though they were pretty

Ms. Sake: 'pretty?!?' they were splendid

Kristin: yeah but i wanted something else but the timing wasn't right

Ms. Sake: yes, it worked out perfect

Ms. Sake: as usual

Kristin: yes it did, it always does

Ms. Sake: thank you

Kristin: thank you

Ms. Sake: i can't tell you how special you make me feel

Ms. Sake: all of the time

Kristin: as you should

Ms. Sake: that's a gift you have

Kristin: because you are

Ms. Sake: no more than you

Ms. Sake: now go

Ms. Sake: go and enjoy the evening

Kristin: i am

Ms. Sake: and especially the moon!

Kristin: 2 more minutes

Kristin: okay, lady and i are heading home, writing some more hoping to wrap this thing up as i am anxious to complete this book ...

Ms. Sake: it's full...like our relationship

Kristin: the moon, yes

Kristin: i have you back for a moment

Kristin: lol

Ms. Sake: yes...and I, for one, cannot wait to read it

Ms. Sake: yeah...I'm so sorry babe
Ms. Sake: I keep getting interrupted
Kristin: you'll enjoy all of it
Kristin: that's okay
Ms. Sake: it's terrible
Kristin: i'm heading out
Ms. Sake: k
Kristin: no worries, you are working
Ms. Sake: have a great night
Kristin: bye you...more later
Kristin: have a great night too
Ms. Sake: you got it
Ms. Sake: i will"

Lady and I drove home. I was writing and decided to send Ms. Sake a text message saying sweet dreams and wishing her a good night. After doing that, I logged onto the Internet, and checked my e-mail, when X-#1 I.M.'ed me, asking if I had ever heard of Ms. Aries, as they are now e-mailing back and forth. I chuckled at this point; not only have I heard of her, she won't leave me alone, and for the first time I put a block on my e-mail from her. She listened to what I had to say, clearly forgetting that we had previously exchanged photos of Ms. Aries. We exchanged pleasantries, and then said good night.

I signed off. I was finishing this book as the time has come to end this diary.

I wanted nothing more than to send Ms. Sake another text message wishing her sweet dreams on this full moon evening. So I sent her another text message and she responded back with the following:

> *"no more last word from u hemmingway, the love is mutual, and always has been! Create knowing the love is mutual, and always has been! Create knowing the universe and I am on your side! Create knowing the universe and I am on your back and your front and on your side and your front and..."*

I responded with the following:

> *"couldn't resist as Hemmingway is my all time favorite, I haven't shared that with you! ...we have some kind of connection, peaceful, calming, amazing, sweet dreams!"*

138

I meant that from the bottom of my heart. I sat listening to a Van Morrison CD, somebody whom I was turned on to many years ago. I hadn't listened to it in a long time. That CD once brought me back to my core, and here I am, many years later, yet on a different level, listening to it again. Everything comes full circle and again there are no coincidences in life; everything happens for a reason.

I am waiting for the next song to play, as this song shall describe my future with Ms. Sake. I will go with it, as I believe in fate. Then it played. The song is called "Just One Love." Song number 8 from the *Best of Van Morrison*. Funny that this was the song that happened to play at that very moment, but not really, as that is what I have found: "That one love, it's ever present everywhere."

The questions are still left to be answered. Is it possible to find true love through Internet dating, and how long will this take if it is possible? It took me 8 months and 17 days to find the answer to that question. Is the Internet a tool that links cyber love with physical love, and an everlasting relationship? Absofuckinglutely!!!

This ends the diary of a lesbian looking for true love. I trust that my lover will accept this part of me, this book, and what true love is all about; accepting people's experiences, differences, and merging both worlds together.

This diary is honest and true, and the story of a lesbian searching for true love, daring to put herself out there, documenting it, and sharing this wonderful experience with the world. Did she find her true love or not over the Internet?

ABOUT THE AUTHOR

Kristin Cranford decided to pursue her lifelong dream of becoming a writer. She was an English major and a lesbian online dater for many years! She currently lives in Los Angeles, CA with her cocker spaniel "Lady."

Printed in the United States
19756LVS00005B/444